the doctor's
redemption

**a
Shadow Creek,
Montana
novel**

the doctor's redemption

a
Shadow Creek,
Montana
novel

VICTORIA JAMES

Entangled Publishing, LLC
2614 South Timberline Road
Suite 109
Fort Collins, CO 80525
Visit our website at www.entangledpublishing.com.

Bliss is an imprint of Entangled Publishing, LLC. For more information on our titles, visit http://www.entangledpublishing.com/category/bliss

Edited by Alethea Spiridon
Cover design by Liz Pelletier
Cover art from iStock

Manufactured in the United States of America

First Edition May 2017

Bliss
an Entangled imprint

Prologue

Dr. Luke Thomson stood amongst a grouping of aspen pines, away from the crowd of mourners, not wanting to be seen, not wanting anything except maybe some closure. But closure didn't come, wouldn't come today, he already knew. It wouldn't be that easy; he didn't deserve for it to be that easy.

Cold, unrelenting November wind and rain battered the Bailey family and their friends as they tried to lay their beloved to rest. It was harsh, violent weather, and it seemed so cruel that they would have to face that too.

He hadn't taken his eyes off any of them, letting their pain sink and seep through him so that he would never forget this moment. Of all the things he'd lived through, the grief and heartache he'd witnessed, nothing compared to what he'd lived this last week. Nothing came close, because he was responsible for all of it.

When his mother was diagnosed with cancer last year, he'd blamed himself. He'd been too busy taking care of his patients to notice the early warning signs. By the time she was diagnosed, a cure wasn't possible anymore. The day he'd told his little sister it was terminal, she had wept all over him, never once blaming him, but he knew it had been his fault. Now they were just waiting for the end.

The night of the accident, the night his wife and unborn baby had died, he'd blamed himself. He was being punished. Their child had been punished. Because of him. He had reached rock bottom. What he'd thought had been hell was nothing compared to the hell he'd have to face moving forward.

His coat flapped with the wind, but he didn't bother buttoning it. He didn't want the shelter, the warmth. The rain mixed with his tears as he watched the caskets being lowered into the earth. The young woman that must have been the mother, wife, stood stoically, exhibiting a control that was admirable and surprising. An older couple flanked either side of her, all of them crying. A tall man, with unflinching, hard features stood behind her, holding an umbrella over her. A young man and woman stood beside one of the parents. The woman didn't lift her head, but from the shaking of her shoulders was crying. The look on the man's face, filled with so much anguish, made it impossible to look away. He had nothing to offer them. There was nothing he could give them today.

When the ceremony was finally over, he didn't move, just observed the crowd of people slowly maneuvering through the muddy cemetery, the rain continuing to torment the mourners. He was unable to move, unable to breathe normally yet. He closed his eyes briefly in an attempt to control his emotions. Acid swirled, unrelenting, in his stomach as he absorbed the impact of his actions on the Bailey family. He'd destroyed two families. Two children.

When he opened his eyes only the woman and the man with the umbrella remained. His gut continued to churn and acid rose in his throat as the woman dropped to her knees.

Her voice echoed throughout the open space, slicing through him, making him never want to look in the mirror again.

He'd go home to spend the last few days with his mother and try to give her some peace. Then he would find a way to start over. He'd begin the journey to finding out what he was made of, what kind of man he could really be, what kind of man he wanted to be. He'd find a way to repent. He'd find a way to look in the mirror again.

But he would be back. He'd be back to face this family.

One day, he'd be back to ask their forgiveness.

Chapter One

Gwen Bailey was in love with the Muffin Man.

She leaned against the white marble counter in her chocolate shop and gazed at the man seated at one of the tables in front of the large bay window. The Muffin Man or TMM as she and her two sisters-in-law now referred to him, came in every day slightly past seven in the morning, shortly after she opened shop. He ordered a large coffee, which he always drank black, and a chocolate chip muffin. He always left a few dollars in the tip jar on the counter and then he'd go and sit at the same table in the window. He usually came in wearing a navy knit hat, with a navy pea coat, and black leather gloves. He always wore a variation of the same clothes-worn-in-all-the-right-places jeans, and a Henley in either grey, navy, or hunter green. He was tall and fit, with broad shoulders and his shirt clung to some very defined biceps.

The Muffin Man read a newspaper. He drank his coffee and ate his muffin in silence. He'd stay for approximately one hour. He always said good morning, thanks, and then gave a wave with what looked like a strong—*ringless*—tanned hand before he left. She knew all this of course, because she'd been secretly drooling over the man for the last few months.

But how was it that she found herself in love with a man she barely knew? Maybe it was the fact that her love life had been non-existent for the last five-going-on-six years. Or maybe it was because it was the most male attention she'd received from a man she wasn't related to in the last five years. Or maybe (and this was the maybe she was hoping for) it was because she sensed a deeper connection with TMM. Maybe she and TMM were meant to be. She created the food he obviously loved to eat.

The only problem with her theory of a deep connection was that he may not be aware of it, because in the two or so months he'd been coming in, he'd never started a conversation. And when she tried to, he usually gave a one or two word answer.

"Uh, hello, what's a pregnant woman gotta do to get a cookie around here?"

Gwen spun around, shocked to see her sister-in-law Lily standing behind her. "What are you doing here?" Gwen always did the morning shift. Lately she'd been doing even more than that to allow her sister-in-law, who also happened to be her BFF and business partner, to plan for the unplanned arrival of twins.

Lily was glowing. She was in her second trimester and Gwen had never seen her look better. It could also have something to do with the fact that Lily and Gwen's brother were now happily married after being apart for five years. "I'm just back from my doctor's appointment and thought I'd give you a hand. I know you've taken on so many of my shifts," Lily said, taking off her red coat and hat, and placing them on a stool behind the counter.

"It's the end of winter, Valentine's long gone. Don't worry, our only customer this morning has been TMM," she said, dropping her voice.

Lily sucked in a breath and clutched Gwen's arm. "TMM is here?"

She nodded excitedly. Because Gwen always did the morning shift, Lily had never met him. Her heart sank as they both looked over to see TMM leaving, his trademark wave-beside-the-head on his way out the door.

"I can't believe I missed him *again*!" Lily said as the door shut behind him. Gwen watched sadly as his tall figure disappeared down the street. She knew that he was going to get into his black Range Rover and drive way…to parts unknown. She had spent way too many hours wondering about that man. Where he drove off to every day. Where he came from every day. It was the longest time until she saw him again.

"Don't worry about it," she mumbled, walking across the empty shop to wipe his table. He had already cleared his garbage. She was starting to feel like a real moron. Her friend was pregnant, married, and here she was obsessing about a man she knew nothing about. A man she had *nicknamed*. How juvenile. "I'd rather hear about your doctor's appointment. What's the latest on the Bailey twins?"

Lily broke out into a huge smile. "Everything's great!" she said, throwing up her arms and looking totally cute with her baby bump and epic glow. "They are both growing well and the doctor has no concerns at all."

Gwen walked across the shop and hugged her friend. "I'm so happy for you and Jack. Have I told you that lately?"

Lily's eyes welled up with tears. "All the time, because you're the best, best friend and sister-in-law and business partner that I could have ever asked for. I never would have thought on New Year's Eve, when I finally saw Jack again, that I'd be standing here a few months later, married and pregnant with baby Jacks," Lily said, full-on tears now making their way down her face.

Gwen reached for the box of tissue they kept on the counter since Lily had found out she was pregnant and cried at the drop of a hat. "Me neither. As a bystander, I'd say it was also pretty fun watching you make Jack pay for leaving you."

Tragedy had struck her family when five years ago, her older brother who was also Jack's twin, had died in a car accident along with their little nephew. Unable to cope, Jack had left town, as had their brother's wife Julia. But now they were all back in Shadow Creek and settled again. Lily and Jack had gotten married in a small but very emotional and touching ceremony a month ago. They were always destined to be together even though things weren't looking very good for her brother a while ago.

Lily smiled sheepishly. "Well, I guess he did deserve it, even if I feel a bit bad now for putting him through the wringer."

Gwen toyed with the front of her apron, anxious to broach a business idea she'd thought up. "Don't worry about it, he deserved it. Listen…I've been thinking about an idea to drum up some business around here during the slow season. What if we did one of those speed dating nights?"

Lily blinked but didn't say anything for a moment.

She knew her friend probably saw right through her pathetic plan. It was kind of out of left field, but business was slow now. She also had no social life. But really, truly, the entire reason was that she wanted a way to lure TMM into a possible date. If he turned her down, then she could once and for all forget her ridiculous crush.

"That's a lot of work, Gwen, and honestly I'm not sure I'm up for it right now. We're still not finished the house reno. Your brother is turning into some crazy nester, insisting we have the place done before the babies. Plus, he's working all the time. Then I don't want to abandon your mom with the baby shower she's planning."

"Julia, my mom, and I are all helping."

"I know, it's just that I already owe you a bunch of hours around here and my extra time I need to spend with Jack and getting organized for not one but two surprise babies. I know that sounds so self-centered. I don't want to say yes and then stiff you with extra work."

She took a fresh chocolate chip cookie off the domed cake stand and handed it to her friend. "No, it doesn't sound self-centered, it sounds honest. I know all the work you have to do over at the house and the baby planning. I get it, the timing totally sucks. Seriously. I don't want you to do anything with this, it'll be my thing." Her timing really did suck; there was no way she could dump this on Lily now. She was just desperate, but of course Lily was focusing on the house and babies. This was something even she, single with no life, could understand.

Lily frowned while taking a large bite of the cookie. "Well, maybe I can find a way."

"Nope. Of course not. I'll totally do this on my own. No extra help required. I'll put up a few signs, add it to our Facebook page and the town's page. Maybe put out an ad in the paper and that's it. It would be a great way to get new people in here."

Lily polished off the cookie and brushed the crumbs off her jacket. "Are you sure speed dating is still a thing? Do they still do those? Wasn't that like a thing in the nineties?"

Gwen rolled her eyes. "This is rural Montana. I'm sure it's just hitting here now."

Lily angled her head. "True…very true. I think it's a great idea, but I've got to help you. Why don't I at least do all the signage, social media posts, and the ad? I can easily do that from home."

Gwen clapped her hands. "Done! I'll do some research on

the best way to run this thing, standard questions to ask and all that stuff, and then send you the details."

"Are you planning on inviting TMM?" Lily asked, wriggling her eyebrows.

Gwen pretended to wipe down the already pristine marble counter to avoid eye contact. "Well, he doesn't really… say much. But I guess it couldn't hurt to invite him. Maybe I'll start by hanging up a poster nonchalantly while he's sipping his coffee. Usually there's no one here that time of morning. Then if he says nothing, I'll casually mention it."

Lily gave a little squeal. "Great idea. So do we know any more about TMM?"

Gwen shook her head. "Nothing. We still haven't spoken about…anything. I've been thinking he's either unemployed or my new career guess for him is woodsman and or lumberjack."

Lily sputtered. "Pardon?"

Gwen stopped wiping and nodded. "I haven't seen him at any of the local businesses."

She could tell Lily was trying not to laugh. "So therefore he must be a woodsman and or lumberjack?"

She crossed her arms. "*No.* But I've thought about this. He also doesn't shave…much. And he's usually dressed very casually, like if he were employed somewhere, he couldn't dress like that."

"Maybe he works from home."

"Yes. As a woodsman and or lumberjack."

"That's not even a job anymore."

Gwen leaned on the counter. "I guess it doesn't really matter. But as I've been sitting here these last two months, I've been doing some soul searching. I've been using everything as an excuse as to why I have no life. Michael and Matthew's death. Helping Mom and Dad. Jack leaving. Julia leaving. But they're all back now. You're all happy. I'm just eating chocolate all day! I want to start living, Lil. I don't want to wait anymore. Life's too short and there are no guarantees," she said, hating that she knew how true that was. Her brother hadn't even been thirty. Her nephew just a toddler. She should learn from that. She needed to be the woman she was meant to be before she was old and living in an apartment with only the truffles they couldn't sell to keep her happy at night.

Tears sprang into Lily's eyes again and she sniffled. "You're right. I'm here for you. Let's do this. Let's get TMM to notice you."

"It doesn't have to be him," she said, lying. *It had to be him.* "Also, if it doesn't work out, then I'm off men. I'd say I need to travel but that's too expensive, so I'll come up with some other fulfilling life plan. Something I'll figure out later."

"It'll work out. This is your time, Gwen. You deserve this. You've been there for everyone else, it's time to focus on your life."

"You're right. I'm done wasting time. I'm going to find someone and I'm going to do it fast."

"Okay. Well, how about some new clothes?"

Gwen looked down at her shapeless black sweater over black leggings. "I guess. I was planning on losing twenty pounds and then going on a shopping spree."

"If I weren't pregnant, I'd threaten to shoot myself if I have to hear about the twenty pounds. If you want to really live, then live now. Don't wait until you reach some goal weight that's only in your head to treat yourself well. If you want to be noticed, then dress for it. Stop hiding. Stop using your weight as an excuse. Also, not that this has to do with going shopping, you did lose weight. Again, let me point out that you don't actually need to lose weight."

"You're the best. Everything you said was true. Yes, I lost a few pounds. Three to be exact. Three miserable pounds that were all blood, sweat, and tears. All I had to do for those three pounds was walk miles every day for the last month. Oh, and I even gave up cream in my coffee. No sugar. I'm drinking black coffee, Lil."

Lily was trying not to laugh, she could tell. "Well, you look great. You always have. This is all in your head. But I'm right when I say you're being too hard on yourself and you need to start living."

Gwen took a deep breath and held up her hands. "You're so right. Fine. New Gwen, new life. Let's go after we close."

Lily beamed. "Perfect, because I need some maternity clothes. I'm bursting out of everything. My wedding dress better fit."

"Of course it will. At least you have an excuse to be bursting out of your clothes. I'm not giving birth to twins," she muttered.

"Gwen," she said sternly.

"Right. Right. Turning over a new leaf."

Lily nodded. "Should I ask Julia if she wants to come?"

Great. Another person to witness her transformation. "Sure, why not!"

• • •

Luke Thomson tried to focus on driving home and not on what had just happened. He had known this day was coming. It was the reason he was in Shadow Creek. But he had no idea that the cute coffee shop girl was Gwen *Bailey*. He'd had his first clue when he'd seen Lily walk in. He had treated her one night in the ER. When she had left the ER it had occurred to him that her fiancé was Jack Bailey.

The Baileys were the people he needed to speak to.

Not that he was interested in a woman, but he'd had a hard time not noticing Gwen this last month. He never would have started going into her shop if he'd known who she was.

It was getting more and more difficult to ignore her though. When he'd first moved to Shadow Creek, there hadn't been any open places to grab a decaf coffee on his way home from the brutal twelve-hour night shift at the hospital. Then he'd noticed this place. The first morning he'd walked in, the sweet smell of freshly baked whatevers and coffee greeted him. But that hadn't been what had hit him in the gut; it had been the gorgeous woman behind the counter. She'd given him a smile that had soothed the turmoil he'd been living with for the last five years. Right from the first, he'd been attracted to her in a way that made her pop into his head throughout the day.

He soon found himself listening to her as she spoke with customers, smiling when he heard her laugh, glancing over at her when she was busy helping people. Everyone who came into her shop loved her. She chatted with them and asked them about their families. She had a way of making each of them feel important and special. Including him. But it was when he'd seen Lily walk in and Gwen refer to her as her sister-in-law that changed everything for him. There would be no asking the gorgeous, sweet, Gwen Bailey on a date. Gwen was off-limits. When she found out who he was, it would destroy her. He could never get close to her or any of them.

He pulled onto the last street before reaching the small cabin he was renting a few miles outside of town. The cabin served its purpose; it was an easy commute to the hospital he worked at, and not that far from town. It was also isolated, which was perfect for him as he had no interest in a social life. That part of his life was long gone and he didn't miss it.

He needed a hot shower and a warm bed.

He pulled into his driveway, frowning when he saw he'd need to shovel the walkway again. His phone rang as he trudged up the front steps. It was his sister.

"Hey, Haley, how are you?" He unlocked the door and walked in, tossing his jacket on the kitchen chair and taking off his boots.

"Okay…" The sigh that followed her "okay" told him everything wasn't okay. He worried about his little sister. He wasn't a worrier in general, but she was the most important person to him, and her marriage last year to a man he totally suspected was a douche, left him apprehensive. Added to that was that she lived three hours from him, so he wasn't able to keep an eye on her. They had grown up together, and being that he was six years older than her, he'd taken on a parental role many times. He'd thought twice about moving to Shadow Creek for the year, but she'd reassured him she would be fine. He also hadn't expected to stay here so long. He hadn't even planned on working, but when he found out how the rural hospital had been in desperate need for doctors, he'd taken on a one year position. In a way, it made the time pass faster as he wasn't a guy accustomed to lying around without anything to do.

"Tell me exactly what's going on," he said, going to his fridge and looking for leftover pizza. He pulled out the box and waited for her answer. Luigi's pizza had saved him many, many nights. It was so good, he ate it cold from the box.

"Are you eating cold pizza?"

He stopped chewing. "No."

"You need to take better care of yourself, Luke."

He continued chewing. "It's vegetarian."

She sighed. "Have you approached the Baileys yet?"

"Haley."

"You're going to have to tell them sooner or later."

He chucked the crust into the open box, his appetite gone. "I know. Maybe tomorrow."

She gasped. "It's going to be okay. It wasn't your fault, Luke."

That was debatable. It didn't matter what the official report said; what mattered is that he felt responsible. He felt like it was his fault and he'd have to carry that burden with him for the rest of his life. He could do that. "Why don't you tell me how your life is going? How's your class of first graders?"

"Great. They're really great. One threw up during story time today. One peed on the rug. It's been a long year."

He almost laughed. He crossed the small cabin and flopped into his bed. "Since that's routine for you, why do you sound so damn sad?"

There was a long pause. He already knew. He also knew his sister was just as stubborn as he was and that meant she wouldn't admit to him if something was wrong, especially since he'd been vocal about her choice of partner.

"I'm not sad. I'm really stressed out. Oh, look at the time, class is going to start again."

His sister usually called him on her break and he knew she had longer to speak. He was too tired to make more conversation anyway. "Fine. I know a crappy excuse when I hear one. Just know this, if you need anything, I'm right here, okay? Don't go being a martyr. You have to get your life back."

He suspected he heard a sniffle. "Okay. But don't worry about me. You've got your own crappy life to worry about."

"Thanks, so happy you called."

She laughed and he smiled.

"Love you, Luke."

"Yeah. Love you too."

He set his phone and wallet down on his nightstand and settled on top of his covers, too tired to bother taking off his jeans or getting under the blankets. As he did most mornings, he pulled out the small photo he carried with him in his wallet. His finger traced the outline in the picture and he said some kind of apology or prayer and then slipped it back in his wallet.

He shut his eyes, hoping for a non-nightmare filled rest.

He wanted one night where he didn't see his wife dead in the seat beside him. One night where he didn't imagine what their unborn baby would have been like had she survived the crash. One night where he could forget that he was the cause of four deaths, and the destruction of two families.

But the last image in his mind, the same once since coming to Shadow Creek, was of Gwen Bailey smiling at him in the morning. He clung to it, wishing like a kid for happy dreams.

Chapter Two

Gwen tried to stuff herself into a dress that was clearly one size too small.

It was her old dress size, but she refused to accept reality, so she insisted on trying it on. Except now reality was staring her back in the mirror of the small change room of the ladies clothing boutique. Her hips looked like they had birthed a dozen children and her boobs looked comically large. She blinked back tears as Mrs. Hastings, the owner, and long-time friend of her mother's, knocked on the door.

"Dear, how's the dress?"

Gwen struggled for words as a dress, two sizes up appeared over the top of the door. Grateful the woman had enough sensitivity not to mention what she'd already known, Gwen took the dress and croaked out a thank-you. She tried to remember what she'd declared to Lily a few hours ago, what she'd promised herself, but it didn't work. Nothing worked. Instead, she started feeling sorry for herself, which she hated. She had rarely done this.

After her brother and nephew had died, she had gotten

a major dose of reality. Real life could suck badly. It could be cruel and unforgiving. Up until the night of the accident, she'd been the sheltered daughter of an upper-middle class, loving family. She'd grown up in a nice house, lived in a beautiful little town, and had been surrounded by wonderful friends and family. But when her brother, Michael, and his little boy, Matthew had died in a car accident, everything had imploded.

Her sweet sister-in-law had left town, her other brother—Michael's twin—Jack had also skipped town, she'd been left to hold her parents together. She had witnessed them broken, and it had killed her to see them so shattered. She'd been forced to be the strong one, and she'd never had to do that before. Sometimes she looked back and wondered how she'd gotten through the days. She didn't know how she'd gotten *them* through the days. Then her father had been diagnosed with cancer and she'd had to take charge of that too—doctor's appointments, treatment, and encouragement.

She'd put on twenty pounds in the process. Twenty pounds of comfort cooking and eating. Oh, but her life was coming back together, because in the last year her family was coming back together. Her sister-in-law Julia had come back for good and was now married to their dear family friend, Chase Donovan. She was thrilled for Julia and knew that Chase and his little girl adored Julia, and they made the sweetest family.

Then there was her brother, Jack. He'd come home on Christmas Eve and all hell had broken loose. But he'd managed to gain everyone's trust again, including the fiancée he left behind five years ago. The two of them were now expecting twins. Gwen and Lily's little chocolate shop was doing great so far.

Everything was great. Really, really, great, except for the fact that she was still trying to be something she wasn't.

Gwen slipped the black dress over her head and stared at her reflection. There was no way the Muffin Man would spare her a second glance, let alone agree to come to her singles night.

"How's that one, dear?"

Gwen shut her eyes and then opened them, hoping for maybe a better reflection in the mirror. It didn't happen. "I'm having trouble deciding today," she said blinking back tears.

There was a knock and then the door opened. Mrs. Hastings took one look at her and shook her head. Great, she also thought Gwen looked horrid. She pursed her lips and yanked Gwen out of the change room and into the store. "My dear, you are doing it all wrong."

"Doing what wrong?" Gwen asked, trying not to make eye contact with Lily and Julia.

Mrs. Hastings stopped in front of a rack of dresses Gwen hadn't even looked at because they were all body-hugging and that was so not what she needed right now. She needed camouflage. The woman pulled out five dresses, draping them on her outstretched arm. She then marched across the room, giving Gwen's body a once-over and then grabbing two pairs of jeans and three sweaters. Gwen didn't say a word as the woman marched over to the lingerie section. Oh God, no.

She ignored Lily's muffled laughter as the woman pulled the measuring tape that was dangling around her neck and started ordering her to lift her arms while she measured her. "You also can't go around wearing grandma underwear. Those sports bras are strapping you down and making you look dowdy."

She broke out into a sweat but stood there like a rag doll as the woman continued to measure her. Oh, the humiliation.

"The first thing you need to attract a man is confidence, not a size two."

She was getting life advice from the elderly owner who was also one of her mother's good friends. "I'm really not trying to attract a man."

Mrs. Hastings gave her a stern look, frowning under her glasses, silently calling her out on her bull, before turning away and quickly rifling through a rack of bras.

Gwen turned to Lily and Julia and mouthed, *I'm going to kill myself.* Lily was silent, laughing so hard she needed to wipe her eyes. Julia turned around.

"Try these on," she said thrusting a handful of lace along with the clothes at Gwen. She had no choice but to accept them. "Now go try on one of those bras under the new clothes and let us decide what looks good and doesn't. Underwire will become your new best friend, dear."

Gwen gave her friends a long look before heading back to the change room. She stood in there and banged her head gently on the door after dropping the clothes on the chair in the corner. What had happened to her? How had this become her life? Why hadn't she just gone online shopping? Right. She would have probably ordered the same old boring clothes. She took a deep breath and rifled through the pile, pulling out an ivory-cashmere-looking sweater that looked way too small for her, and some dark blue skinny jeans she never would have even attempted wearing. She groaned out loud as she picked up a bra. It was two sizes larger than the size she normally wore.

"Gwen, hurry up, I'm starving and need to eat dinner!"

"I will try to hurry and not jeopardize the growth of my future nephews or nieces!" she yelled. She heard their laughing but focused on the display in the change room. Gwen didn't want to offend her mother's friend but there was no way any of those clothes were going to look good on her. Maybe twenty pounds ago… "Mrs. Hastings, I appreciate your effort, but I'm not feeling it today."

"Nonsense. Put the clothes on. And then come out after you try on each so that I can see."

Gwen frowned at her through the door. "I really don't

think…"

"Now."

"Yeah," said her traitorous best friends. "Now."

Mrs. Hastings knocked on the door.

"I haven't even gotten dressed yet," she said, trying not to sound as irritated as she felt.

"Precisely. I didn't want to say anything, and I'm certainly not one for gossip, but I think you need to hear this before you try those clothes on. I know you come from a long line of stubborn, Gwen, so I think you need more convincing. I haven't even told this news to your mother yet."

Gwen reluctantly opened the door.

Mrs. Hastings had taken off her glasses now and they were dangling by a red chain on her chest. "You know my daughter-in-law, Brianna?"

Gwen nodded slowly, dread forming in her stomach as tears filled the older woman's eyes. Brianna was Jack's age and they had gone to school together but now lived a few towns away. She hadn't seen her in a while.

"Well, she found out she has breast cancer. She's only in her thirties and has two small children. That poor woman is going to have to have a double mastectomy, chemo, and radiation."

Gwen gasped. "I'm so sorry to hear that," she whispered. Her stomach churned at the thought of what Bri was now facing. "She's going to be okay though, right?"

"Yes," Mrs. Hastings said with a forceful nod. Gwen caught the tremble in her chin and the sheen in her eyes and threw her arms around the woman.

"She will be. She will be fine. Let me know what I can do to help. Please tell her I'm here for her," she said, not thinking twice about offering her help.

"I will tell her, dear. Thank you. But now hear my words—enjoy your life. Be proud of who you are. This obsession we all have with our appearance and our obsession with looking a certain way isn't right. Appreciate that you are here on earth, Gwen. You are a beautiful woman and it doesn't matter what size you are. I'm not judging you. I'm saying all this to you because I know you're such a good person. I know what kind of a daughter you've been to your parents. You deserve happiness, Gwen. Any man would be lucky to have you. Just hold out for a good one, dear. You don't want to get a lemon."

Lily was sobbing as she came over and passed around the box of tissues to all of them.

God, she'd never felt so low or so shallow. The things she had been worrying about? Not real problems. "I'm so sorry for Brianna. If there's anything I can do, please tell me."

Mrs. Hastings gave her a kiss on the cheek and wiped her own tears. "Thank you, my dear. Now, let's get you looking alive again."

Gwen nodded, walking back into the changing room. This was the moment she was going to change for good. She had learned her lesson. She had learned so many lessons these past few years. It was high time to act on them.

• • •

Gwen hung up the phone, pleased that both her sisters-in-law were on board with her latest plan. After her shaming yesterday, she had found Brianna's email and reached out to her. Gwen offered to bring her dinner for the family every Friday night. When she told Lily and Julia about her plan, they both said they'd contribute as well on some weeks. Her mother had also agreed.

Gwen pressed the brew button on the coffeemaker inside the chocolate shop and then arranged the morning's baked goods on their appropriate stands. Her heart raced as it usually did because she knew TMM would be arriving momentarily.

She sat down at the stool behind the counter, very pleased. She felt reenergized. She jotted down some meal ideas on a napkin and then took out her planner. Her to-do list was getting longer and longer. There was all the baby shower stuff, plus, her parents had some doctor's appointments coming up and she always made a point of driving them and attending. And of course, now there was the speed dating. She was completely engrossed in her planning until she realized it was past the Muffin Man's usual time. She glanced at the oversized antique clock hanging in the chocolate shop for what had to be the tenth time in half an hour. The Muffin Man should have been there five minutes ago.

She was dressed…like a normal person again. She also felt like a normal person again. She was taking charge today, putting her plan into effect. She was wearing one of her new outfits and she was doing it with confidence. She had to admit she felt good. It felt good to rid herself of the stupid limitations she'd placed on herself. This was day two in the beginning of the new Gwen. As soon as she closed the shop tonight, she was planning on hanging up some of the cute posters she'd printed on the community bulletin boards like at the library and recreation centers. She was waiting until TMM was here to hang up the store poster. If she was feeling extra kick-ass, she was going to invite him to attend.

Yesterday's experience had been eye-opening. She was done with feeling sorry for herself, she was done with self-loathing. She was done with needing to lose twenty—well, seventeen—pounds to find happiness. She was going to live in gratitude for what she had—boobs, hips, and a butt. At least she had them.

She quickly shuffled her stack of speed dating flyers and shoved them to the far side of the counter as the jingling bells on the front door told her the first customer of the day was arriving. Her first customer was always TMM. Sure enough, tall, dark, and oh-so-handsome, TMM was walking through the door. He looked tired this morning. His classic stubble looked as delectable as ever, but she could see the lines around what she thought was a very sensual mouth on a very hard-lined masculine face, looked more pronounced today. His brilliant, Montana-sky blue eyes, had dark circles under them. She adjusted her new ivory V-neck fake cashmere sweater over her dark skinny jeans and wondered if TMM would look at her differently today.

"Good morning!" she said in her brightest voice. Her heart was beating rapidly, looking for some sign of…interest.

"Morning," he said as he walked in. TMM's voice was sort of like rich, dark chocolate and it always seemed to filter through her body, warming her on the inside.

"Cold out there, isn't it?"

"Yeah."

She poured his coffee and gave him his usual muffin, and he laid out the exact change. He walked away while her mouth was still open, ready to continue the conversation. He hadn't done a double take at her in her new clothes, makeup, or actual combed hair today either. She would not be deterred. It was a minor setback, that was all.

She watched him covertly, thinking up her next move. She'd hang the flyer on the community board above the cream/sugar/coffee station right when he was about to leave. He always cleared his table before leaving—another totally endearing quality. The jingle on the door prompted her to look like a normal merchant and not a stalker. She groaned inwardly as Marlene Mayberry, town mayor, eternal busybody walked in, followed by the rest of the morning crowd. It was time for this day to begin. She began filling orders, soon losing track of TMM's actions.

"I hear there's a baby shower coming up, Gwen. I'll be sure to look for my invitation in the mail!" Marlene said as she lingered at the display counter, trying to decide between a muffin and the new homemade chocolate protein bars they were carrying. Gwen already knew, based on her ordering history, the muffin would win out.

"Well, we still have loads of time," Gwen said, standing in front of the muffin stand, tongs ready. Marlene always asked about what was happening in their lives — well, anyone's lives.

"Wonderful, wonderful. How about you, dear? Any plans on walking down the aisle soon?" she asked as she finally pointed to the muffins.

Gwen gritted her teeth and forced a smile. "Nope, just taking my time, enjoying being single."

Marlene handed her the exact change since she always ordered the same thing. "Well, don't wait too long. One day you'll be in your twenties and the next you'll wake up and realize you're forty!"

"I don't think Gwen has anything to worry about, Marlene." She looked up to find Ben Matthews leaning against the counter. Firefighter Ben. Hot Firefighter Ben who'd dated Lily for a while. He had nicknamed Gwen "Sweets" in high school, and he continued to use the nickname now, years later. She had no complaints. She would have entertained dating Ben since she knew nothing happened between him and Lily, except for the fact that there was a brooding, mysterious woodsman who had captured her interest. Now Ben, with his easy smile, dark, disheveled hair, tall, hot body — not to mention heroic profession — just didn't do it for her. The spark was missing. The spark she felt whenever her hand brushed TMM's as she handed him his mug of coffee.

Marlene was all flustered and smiling at Ben, completely forgetting her doomsday forecast for Gwen. Once she'd sputtered off, he turned to Gwen.

"Morning, Sweets."

"Good morning, Ben! You came in at the perfect time. I

was ready to pluck my eyeballs out with the tongs."

He laughed. "No problem. No one needs advice from Marlene, especially in the morning."

"So true," she said. "How are things with you?'

"Good, just busy at work. You're looking especially beautiful this morning." She paused as she filled up a paper cup of his usual coffee. He noticed. Why did *he* notice and TMM didn't even give her a second glance?

"Well thank you," she said, handing him his order. "Listen, um, I'm holding a speed dating night next week. Would you be interested in attending?"

The look on his handsome face told her clearly that no, he would not be interested. He pushed himself off the counter and sighed. "If you're hosting, then yeah. I'll be here."

"Ah!" She clapped her hands. "Thank you so much! Here and here," she said, handing him a chocolate chip cookie and then a flyer. "It's on the house."

He laughed. "Thanks, Gwen. You know, the only reason I'm even entertaining a speed dating night is because you'll be there."

She wished she had feelings for him, and not the loner who was sitting with his head buried in the newspaper.

• • •

Luke lowered the newspaper and tried to not look like he was watching Ben the Moron Firefighter. Seriously, he didn't get the appeal of that guy. He also didn't like that he was after Gwen…*stop thinking like that, Luke.* You're not after Gwen. Gwen can have her own life. Besides, Gwen would one day hate him when she found out the truth, so for the both of them he needed to stay away.

Luke tried not to scowl as firefighter extraordinaire, according to the blabbering mayor, sauntered over to Gwen.

He also tried not to scowl into his newspaper after she laughed at one of his undoubtedly dumb jokes.

That Ben guy was always lurking around. Always cheerful. Always making Gwen laugh.

A real loser.

He pretended to be looking out the window, but was just trying to catch their reflection and see what the life-saving loser was up to. He was currently leaning against the counter as though his legs were too weak to support him. His gut churned when he saw him pick up one of those red flyers Gwen had stacked on the front counter. Of course Ben would be available.

He did grin when he heard the mayor ask if her single adult children could attend. Ben and Gwen were stumbling over their words and he guessed her kids were just as obnoxious as she.

Just when he thought he was going to leave, he spotted Ben jotting something down on a red flyer, something that might be a phone number. Dammit. This was not supposed to bother him. What, because he couldn't have Gwen no one could? None of this should matter to him. He was relieved nonetheless when Ben walked—swaggered—out of the shop followed by the loud mayor. The place was now almost empty again and he forced himself to focus on the newspaper. Not that he was interested, he just didn't feel like leaving Gwen yet.

He stared through bloodshot eyes at the newspaper, or tried to anyway. He was going to force himself to do just that, and not check out whatever new look Gwen was sporting today. He'd known the moment he'd walked into this place months ago that she was gorgeous. He'd been attracted to her immediately. Like, the kind of attraction that sent his blood pumping and his thoughts wandering to places they shouldn't be. But today…she was a whole new level of hot.

Against his better judgement, he lifted his eyes from the headlines he'd had to reread five times this morning, and glanced over at what she was doing. She was currently hanging some red paper on the bulletin board that was hung over the cream/sugar/coffee station. It was too far away for him to read what it was, but he wasn't interested in the sign. It was Gwen that he was interested in. Or checking out this new version of her. She was wearing a pair of body-hugging skinny jeans that highlighted a very cute ass and a sweater that clung to spectacular breasts that he'd already suspected were hiding under the baggy clothes she usually wore.

He shifted uncomfortably in his seat and tried to refocus on the miserable daily news. Except his coffee was done. The paper was pretty much read, the good sections anyway, and he'd inhaled the muffin an hour ago. Yeah, it was time to go, time to get on with his usual routine. He'd drive back to his rented cabin, dress for a winter jog, go back home, shower, and then sleep until two hours before his next shift started.

He stood, glancing over to make sure Gwen wasn't still at the coffee creamer station and gathered his plate and cup. He eyed the red flyer she'd been pinning up, wishing he was wearing his glasses. But as he approached he made out the headline: FINDING LOVE WITH THE CHOCOLATIERS! Once he dumped his garbage, he read the sign closely, a sinking feeling in his gut. It looked like Gwen was hosting a speed dating night at the shop. That's what that firefighter had been blabbing about. Did that mean she was looking for someone? The firefighter?

"Are you free next Friday night?"

Crap. He hadn't heard her approach. He turned to look down at the cute brunette he'd been avoiding for weeks. Standing this close to Gwen only intensified what he'd been trying to ignore. Up close her eyes were the color of fine brandy, her skin flawless and smooth…and her mouth was the most kissable he'd ever seen. *Stop it right there, man.* Time to leave. He coughed. "I work nights."

The disappointment across a face that had been so hopeful made him feel like an ass. It also confirmed what he'd already suspected—their attraction was mutual. Hell, that only made things worse.

"Well..."

"I'd better get going. Thanks for the food. Good luck with the event."

He turned and gave her a wave before leaving the shop.

Good luck with the event? What a prick he was. So fine, he'd rather have some plague than attend a speed dating night, but it killed him to say no to her.

His day was always downhill from here, always downhill from when he left her.

Chapter Three

"So, TMM has blatantly rejected me." Gwen took a sip of wine and waited patiently for words of sympathy from her sisters-in-law.

Julia sat back in the comfy booth at The Mountainside Inn for one of their weekly get-togethers, and narrowed her eyes on her. "I don't believe you. Did you ask him out? Tell me right from the beginning exactly how this all went down."

Sheesh. "Have you been taking lessons from Chase on how to interrogate people?"

Julia and Lily laughed. "I think we know you have a flair for the…dramatic, so we just want to get all the details so we can accurately assess the situation," Lily said.

They paused as a platter of loaded nachos and another platter of tortillas and artichoke dip was placed on the table. "Oh, this is exactly what I need," Gwen said, eying the food. "Because, really, I might as well eat my way into a coma since the only guy I'm interested in rejected my invitation."

"Okay. Begin. Leave out no details," Julia said, grabbing a chip and dipping it.

Gwen didn't even have an appetite. She watched her sisters-in-law dive into the food. "I had just finished hanging up the speed dating flyer and then he came up to toss out his garbage and I caught him looking at the sign...so then, because I've decided to be more assertive and go after what I want, I asked him if he was free Friday night." Her face was inflamed just thinking about the humiliation when he basically turned his back and walked out of the shop.

"And?" Julia asked.

"He said no!" She grabbed her wine glass and gulped a few times.

Lily held a loaded nacho close to her lips. "He just said no?"

Gwen sighed and hunched forward, eyeing her now empty glass of merlot. "He said he's working."

"That's not the same as rejecting you!" Julia yelled, a little too loudly, judging by the glances they drew from nearby tables.

"Agreed. What's the man supposed to do?" Lily added, grabbing more food. "Quit his job?"

Gwen rolled her eyes and eyed the artichoke dip. "He could have said that we could go out one night or...anything. He just walked away and did that wave I once thought was endearing but now find infuriating." She stabbed a chip into the dip.

"Maybe he's shy," Julia said.

"No, I've already entertained that possibility. He doesn't strike me as shy. He's...quiet. Not shy. There's a difference. It's like he's choosing not to speak rather than feeling too shy to speak." She stuffed the loaded chip into her mouth.

Julia frowned and pointed a chip in her direction. "What's his job?"

Gwen shrugged and slumped down in her seat. "I have no idea."

Lily groaned. "You didn't ask?"

Gwen threw up her arms. "He walked away. I wasn't going to go chasing after TMM."

Julia paused the conversation to order another bottle of wine for the table. "Does TMM have a name?"

"No...but I know his car. What if I wrote down his license plate number? Do you think Chase would look him up for me?"

They both paused and looked at her. That's when it dawned on her—she was pathetic and juvenile. This TMM thing had gone on long enough. "You know what? Don't answer that. I'm done with the Muffin Man. Done. I will meet someone at my stupid singles night. Clearly TMM and I aren't meant to be. He didn't even look at me...in any way and I was wearing my new cute clothes." She didn't add how disappointed she'd been. She'd felt stupid. She'd taken extra time with her hair again that morning, had bothered with mascara and the whole thing. She'd worn her cute clothes, even her cute bra. He hadn't even given her a second glance.

"I'm not going to say to give up on him, but I think you should be open to the guys you meet next Friday. You could meet some great guys. Who knows, you might even have trouble choosing which one you want to date first!" Lily said.

"I don't want anyone else."

Julia drank the last sip of wine. "If it's meant to be, it's meant to be. If not, I have someone perfect in mind for you. He's a realtor I met last week."

Gwen held up her hand. "I'm going to stop you right there, no set ups."

Julia reached for the wine bottle. "He's a really great guy."

This was what she'd been dreading. The pitying set up attempts by her friends. Not going to happen. Gwen frowned and eyed Julia and her wine glass. "What's with the wine consumption?"

Her face turned the color of red they'd just consumed. "Nothing…"

"So bad at lying," Lily said with a laugh. "Out with it."

Tears suddenly appeared in her eyes. "Okay, don't say anything, but as of Monday, Chase and I are going to almost maybe start trying for a baby."

Lily and Gwen reached across the table and hugged their friend, knowing what a huge leap this was for her. They were all laughing and crying. "I'm so happy for you," she whispered.

"Me too. We'll be pregnant at the same time!" Lily said.

Julia toyed with the stem of her wine glass. "Well, we're not actually trying. We decided to not prevent anything from happening."

"I'm sure Chase thinks he'll have you pregnant next month," she said with a laugh.

Julia rolled her eyes. "He did say something exactly like that. But listen, let's talk some baby shower stuff. I was at Cassy and Edward's last night and we're thinking we can easily set up the buffet we'd planned in their dining room. So tomorrow how about we all meet and select the rentals, linens, and flowers?"

Lily hugged Julia. "Thank God for you two. I feel pulled in so many different directions and I can barely focus on the planning."

"We've got your back," Gwen said. Speaking of which she needed to add to her shower to-do list.

"So does Maggie. She's insisting on coming with us."

They all laughed again. Everyone had found a new way to live after the tragedy they were all connected by. They had found a new path, a new way to happiness. Except for her. She was still drifting, still figuring out who she was now. Who she was beyond the girl who had to be strong enough to pick up the pieces, to pick up her family when they were down. She needed to stop being the one without a life. Or at least she needed to stop looking like the one with no life.

• • •

Luke tried to pull the door to The Chocolatiers open, but was surprised when it wouldn't budge. He frowned, glancing down at his watch. Gwen was always open by now. The sign was flipped to OPEN and the lights were on inside. He peered through the door and didn't see any sign of her. Usually she was behind the counter.

Just go home. He knocked on the door. When she still didn't appear, he banged on it with his fist. Seconds later, she emerged from the kitchen, confusion stamped across her gorgeous face. Now that Gwen had this new look going on, he enjoyed seeing what her new clothes would be for the day. Not that he cared about her clothing selection, it was more about the way she looked in them. Today he couldn't see much because she had a pink Chocolatiers apron on top of some dark jeans. Her hair was up in a knot, her face looked flushed, and her lips were a pretty, very kissable red.

She unlocked the door and swung it open. "I'm so sorry! I totally thought I had unlocked this. I'm in the back working on a few things," she said, talking while she walked behind the counter. She immediately started pouring his coffee.

"No worries," he said, trying not to check out her cute butt while she continued talking and filling his order.

"It's been so crazy around here and I thought I'd get in here early to knock a few items off my to-do list, but instead I'm making a total disaster," she said, finally standing still and looking at him. The muffin was on a plate and his coffee in a cup.

He liked hearing her speak. Gwen had an energy about her that was contagious. In another lifetime he would have wanted in on that. She was bubbly without being irritating.

"Well, hope it works out for you." He was an ass. That wasn't what he wanted to say, but if he said what he wanted to say, things would take a totally new direction and he couldn't have that. Bad enough he let himself come in here every day.

He placed his money on the counter, grabbed his order and walked to his table, not before seeing the disappointment flicker in her brown eyes. He sat at his usual spot and once again pretended that the newspaper was more important than whatever it was that Gwen was up to. He heard the swinging of the kitchen door and knew that she'd gone back in there.

What had to be fifteen minutes later, while he was deep into the Sports section, he heard lots of crashing followed by loud cursing. He sighed and ignored it. More crashing. More cursing. He stretched out his legs. *You can't go back there, Luke. Sit still.* It was when he heard the giant crash that he decided he couldn't just sit there any longer. He made his way to the back and pushed the swing door open and assessed the situation in front of him. Gwen was standing over what looked like a pile of dessert, her eyes filled with tears.

"Uh, you okay?" he asked. Since he'd spent the last month or so trying not to talk to Gwen, he noticed he came across somewhat like a Neanderthal.

She crouched down in front of the food and picked up a large piece of what he could now tell was pie. "I'm fine. You can go back to your coffee."

Don't spend time with her. You checked up on her, she's fine. Go sit.

He walked forward and crouched down in front of her, eyeing the pie. "That sucks."

She sighed and looked up at him. He quickly looked down at the pie because sitting this close to Gwen, looking at Gwen was dangerous. Her eyes made him uncomfortable. They held so many secrets and so many truths. He read the interest in them daily, but it was nothing he could act on so it just made him miserable.

"Yeah, you don't know the half of it. I have spent a week trying to get this recipe right. It's a low-carb, sugar-free pie recipe that I'm trying to surprise my pie-addicted, prediabetic, father with," she said, standing.

He joined her at the counter. "It looks good. Smells good too."

She shrugged. "Yeah. Do you want to try?"

He looked down at the piece she was holding, the glass pie plate under it.

"Don't worry, there's no glass in here. I think."

He couldn't help but grin. "Death by pie. I'm willing to take the risk."

Her eyes lit up and something inside him came alive for the first time in a long time. He took the piece and sampled it. "It's really good," he said. The warm blueberries were tart and sweet at the same time and the crust was moist and slightly dense.

"Oh, good. It's an almond flour crust and I used maple syrup as the sweetener."

"It's really good," he said, swallowing the last bite.

"Great." Before he was done chewing, she was sweeping up the mess and then moving onto the island and shuffling some dishes around. "Do you like homemade mac'n'cheese?" she asked.

"Considering your muffin is the only homemade thing I eat, I'll say yes," he said, walking over to join her.

"Then here," she said, handing him a small bowl and fork. "There's nothing wrong with it, it was just too much to fit in the casserole dish."

He loaded his fork with as much of the gooey looking macaroni as possible and then ate it. It was like heaven in his mouth. "That's pretty damn good," he said in between mouthfuls. "Why do you have so much food?"

"Oh," she said, while she wrapped aluminum foil over two large casserole dishes. "It's for a sick friend. I need to deliver them after work."

He stopped chewing for a second, her statement reminding him of the kind of people the Bailey's were. They were good people. People who helped others. People who loved. He finished the last piece and then put his bowl and fork in the sink. "Thanks, uh, for the food."

He walked out of the kitchen, knowing he was being rude, but knowing it was for the best.

Chapter Four

Stupidest idea ever? Hosting a speed dating night. *What* had she been thinking?

She would never, ever, in a million years date any of these guys. Gwen looked out at the filled chocolate shop and wondered what had ever possessed her to think this would be a good idea. She hated being judgemental, but she already had a nickname for each one of them. There was the Nerd, no explanation needed. Then there was the Narcissist, the Sexist, the Shyboy, the Mamasboy, the Know-it-all, and the Boobstarer.

She felt awful for the women who came here tonight too—until she saw them all hooking up and leaving her standing in the middle of her shop alone! So, great. The only normal guy that said he would be here—Ben—got called into work so she was forced to deal with this crowd on her own.

And of course, the Muffin Man was MIA.

She shouldn't be surprised. After yesterday's weird encounter in the kitchen, she should know not to count on him. First he barged back into the kitchen like he was ready to rescue her from a fire, then he turned all indifferent again—except when he inhaled all the food. He looked totally fine then. And after he inhaled all the food, he just disappeared.

The wind howled outside and snow was falling in large gusts. She didn't even care. Usually late March snowstorms drove her crazy, but it felt rather perfect tonight. She watched the last of them leave and then locked up behind them. She wiped the tables one by one and tried not to cry. What was wrong with her? How hard was it to find a decent guy? She had been alone for so long. Was she so repulsive that even the dolts that were here tonight weren't interested in her? She didn't know how much longer she could wait. Her only other option would be to leave town. Maybe it was lack of men that was the problem. Maybe she needed a city, but she couldn't leave Shadow Creek. She loved it here. She was too attached to her family, even though they drove her nuts. No, no. Her life was full. She didn't need a man. Maybe her obsession with the Muffin Man was because he was unattainable. She knew nothing about him. He could be a crazed lunatic. She needed to stop that obsession. Maybe she should go out with Ben, but no, she didn't want to lead him on.

Gwen finished wiping the tables and then turned off the remaining lights. It was time to call it a night. She'd go back to her apartment down the street, put on flannel pj's, and drink herself to bed. Then tomorrow when she woke up, she'd continue on this new path she'd set out for herself. The new Gwen wasn't insecure and she was going to make sure the new Gwen wasn't lonely either.

• • •

Luke leaned his head back against the headrest and swore out loud in his empty car. He felt like a stalker. He'd told Gwen he wouldn't come to her singles night—and he had many valid reasons.

First, he'd rather die than attend something like that. Second, he was supposed to be working tonight. Third…he didn't want to be in a position where he'd be close to her. Gwen was off-limits to him. He already knew he was very attracted to her and that it was mutual. He already knew she was funny, sweet, and…hell, this was bad. But the crushed look on her pretty face had made him request the night off — which was something he never did. He was planning on sitting in his car and making sure she was fine. You could never be too careful. Jerks were everywhere.

He wanted her to find someone tonight. Well, a part of him did. The other part didn't want her to find anyone but him, but he did know that he didn't want to see her cry, and he knew that was what was happening now. He'd also seen all the other losers leave, paired off in couples. Through the blustery snow outside his car, he could see her blowing her nose as she cleaned up the place. He spotted her yanking down the red flyer and tearing it to shreds. It confirmed what he'd already suspected — that tonight was about her finding someone. The way she'd looked at him when she asked him if he'd come tonight replayed in his mind over and over. He had no idea how he'd said no to her, which again was why he had said no to her. Dammit.

He had no idea how any of those guys wouldn't have wanted her. She looked stunning, even from across the road he could tell. She was wearing a body-hugging red dress, black leather high-heeled boots, and some little black too-small cardigan. Her hair was piled on top of her head and a few pieces dangled down.

His gut clenched when she sat down at a table and put her head in her hands and he saw her shoulders shaking. Hell.

He was going in.

He got out of his car, swore because the storm was blowing

gusts of wind and snow in his face, and then jogged across the street. Downtown Shadow Creek was a ghost town at the moment because of the late hour and the storm. Huge drifts had formed and he hadn't seen a plow out in hours. His gut tightened as he reached the door to her shop and noticed she hadn't picked up her head yet. He knocked on the door and she sat up with a start, wiping her eyes with a napkin before turning and standing. She stopped dead in her tracks when she spotted him. Her eyes and nose were red, her hair was now all messed up, but as she walked toward him, he knew she was still the most beautiful woman he'd ever known.

She unlocked the door, her brows furrowed, her lips drawn into a frown, as she opened it and let him in. "It's not morning. I don't have any coffee or muffins ready." She then tried to shut the door on him.

Well, genius, what's your plan? You didn't want to see her cry, so now what? "I didn't come for the muffins." So now he was creeping her out because it was nighttime, her shop was empty, and he was looming over her. What was he going to say? He had been stalking her from across the street?

"Oh." She blew her nose again and crossed her arms.

"Can I come in?"

She nodded and moved aside. "Right. Sorry. So why are you here?"

Why was he here… "I was driving by and saw the lights were on and you looked like you were crying."

Her eyes narrowed on him. "I thought you were working tonight."

"I got off early."

"Oh. I wasn't crying. I have allergies sometimes."

He'd never seen her blow her nose once in the last few months that he'd been coming here. "Oh. Okay, well, if you're fine then…"

She started tapping her foot which then prompted him

to notice those boots again, after an appreciative perusal of her body as his gaze made its way down. He wasn't prepared for the hot Gwen look. Just as he was about to leave, relieved that she looked pissed rather than sad, the lights flickered and then went out. "What the hell?"

They stood there, in darkness, watching as the entire town went to black.

"Oh, crap. It's the stupid storm," she said, her voice sounding slightly panicked. "It's so dark in here. Omigod, I don't even have a flashlight. Ah! But I have all the votive candles from this stupid singles night."

"Do you know where they are?"

"Yup. Matches are behind the counter. You stay there, I know my way around this place," she said.

"Are you okay?" he asked, wincing when he heard her crash into something.

"Yup! No worries at all."

He heard another crash, some muffled swearing, then the whisper of a match being lit. He took one of the tea lights once it had been lit and helped her light them. In a few minutes there was enough light in the shop that they could make out their surroundings. This wasn't good. Candlelight. A storm. And the one woman he wanted but couldn't have. He couldn't exactly leave her here like this. "Do you live close to here?" he asked.

"Walking distance. Down the street, actually. I took over my sister-in-law's place when she moved out last month."

"Can I walk you home?"

"Do you live in town?"

"'Bout a half hour out."

She looked beyond his shoulder. "I don't think you're going to make it home."

He turned around to look out the window. His SUV was buried in snow. "It's pretty good in the snow."

"Usually the roads get shut down when we have a storm like this."

He shoved his hands in the front pockets of his jeans.

"Well, as long as you're not insane or anything, you can stay at my place if you'd like," she said, walking around the counter to grab her coat. He made sure to not be noticeably checking out the sway of her hips and how good she looked in the dress that clung to everything wonderful.

He couldn't go home with Gwen. He had told himself not to get involved with her. In his defense, when he'd first moved to Shadow Creek, he'd had a plan, he was focused. He'd walked into this little shop because it'd been the only place serving coffee early in the morning after his shift at the hospital. He hadn't counted on the owner being one of the people whose lives he destroyed. He hadn't counted on wanting to see her smile every day. But going home with her would only make the truth so much harder when it came out. God, he hated his life.

"You know what?" she interrupted the silence, and he looked over at her, all bundled up now and marching toward the door like a woman with a bone to pick. He had no idea what he'd done to piss her off since he hadn't spoken…

"I don't get you. You look like a guy who has a lot to say, yet you say nothing. You show up every day and barely say a word to me, but you have these…" She paused for a second, came up to him and waved her hand in front of his face. "These wounded eyes that make me feel like you need a friend. Then because you're basically the only guy who… is mildly attractive, I ask you to this stupid singles night that I will never do again unless I have an early death wish, and you say no. Well, now you're here, in a blizzard, barely saying a word and I invite you to stay at my place and all you can do is stand there…looking like that?" She waved a hand in front of him again.

"Gwen."

Her mouth dropped open. "You know my name?"

He tried to fight the smile, he tried to fight the feeling, the attraction. He could. He totally could be in the same room with this woman, in the dark, and not make a move. He shouldn't have taken a step forward, then. "I've been here every day except Sunday for over a month."

"Right," she said, her voice suddenly breathless. This was going to end badly. "I don't know your name."

"I believe you do."

She shook her head and another piece of her dark hair tumbled out. He flexed his hand, telling himself not to touch. "No, I really don't."

"I think I'm the Muffin Man. Or TMM."

She slapped a hand across her mouth, her eyes wide as saucers. "Omigod."

He was done fighting the grin. She was pretty damn hilarious. "Yeah. Your voice has a tendency to carry."

Her hands covered her face now and she groaned. He laughed, and then he broke his first rule and reached out to touch her; he tried to pry her hands off her face and succeeded after a few seconds. He didn't want to let go and she didn't make a move to take her wrist from his hand. Dammit. She was looking up at him with those whiskey-colored eyes filled with the unmistakable sheen of attraction. "Okay, Muffin Man, then tell me what you're really doing here tonight." Her voice was soft and breathy, but the challenge was in it.

He didn't want her to go home with someone else. If he told her that, they'd be starting something. He couldn't start something with Gwen Bailey. He owed the Baileys an apology, not this. Except she took a step into him, a challenge in her eyes, in the tilt of her chin. Ah, hell. As if he'd ever refuse her, and he'd always been one to walk into a challenge.

He had amazing self-control and self-discipline. He could

kiss her once and then walk away, maybe then he'd get her out of his system. Maybe it was just attraction to a woman unlike any other he'd ever been with. But he couldn't get involved with her.

He shoved his hands in his pockets, because if not, he was going to pull her close. "I didn't want you to go out with some guy from speed dating."

Her eyes widened. "Really?"

He gave a quick nod. He hated lying. The truth wasn't so great either.

"Would you say you find me somewhat attractive?"

Somewhat? He gave another nod. He had no idea where she was going with this.

"Are you married or dating someone?"

"Nope."

She gave him a huge smile. "Great. Then you can take me out on a date next week."

He coughed. Choked, really. "Excuse me?'

She nodded. "Yup. I think you'll be perfect."

"You…can't get a date?"

Her face turned red. "Of course I can. I just happen to be very picky. You seem like someone I would date."

Oh, man. He hadn't seen this one coming. He couldn't date Gwen, and why couldn't she find a date? Any of those losers he'd seen in here would have been lucky to have her. "I can't date you."

Her smile dipped and a flash of insecurity dashed across her incredible eyes. "Why?"

His gut tightened. He caught the faint tremor in her voice. Crap. As long as there weren't tears in her eyes he'd be fine. He'd caused this woman enough tears. He searched for the right words. Finally, he came up with, "I don't think we're right for each other." There. That wasn't insulting. It also wasn't lying, but it was firm.

Her chin trembled again, but then she squared her shoulders and lifted her chin. "Oh, like as in, I'm not your type? You wouldn't date *me*?"

Uh-oh. It was as though he was falling into some deep, dark hole of female double speak that he was not programmed to understand. It was like there was an entirely different conversation playing in her head. He was about to tell her that he didn't mean it like that when she continued speaking.

"Never mind. I wouldn't date you either. I barely even remember your order. It's not like I know anything about you. Actually, I vaguely even remember you. Are you that guy who comes in here every morning and mumbles out an order and then proceeds to ignore me for an hour and then leaves with a rude wave? The guy who stuffs pie samples and mac and cheese and then takes off?"

Hell. He scraped a hand down the side of his face.

She put her hands on her hips. "So what is your type exactly?"

Her. She was his type. He took a step into her when he should have just turned around and left after reassuring her that the problem was with him, not her. Except he'd wanted her since the day he'd walked into this little chocolate shop and first laid eyes on her. His attraction to her had only grown, and now she was here asking him to be her date and asking him why he wasn't attracted to her.

"Never mind," she said making a little shooing motion with her hand. Now he'd really pissed her off. "Just go. I've had enough of this one-sided conversation anyway."

He grabbed her wrist when she turned to walk away. "Gwen," he said roughly.

She stilled and looked up at him.

He'd regret this later, he already knew.

He smiled and took a step into her, letting go of her wrist. He heard her breath catch and blood started pumping through his veins. She leaned her head back and it took all of his self-control not to kiss her.

"I notice you. I notice everything about you. I know that this entire town loves you. I know you sneak a chocolate muffin in the morning and eat it bit by bit while you're serving customers. I know you only charge that old guy with the beard half the actual price of his breakfast order. I know you hate tea even though you pretend to know what you're talking about when customers ask you your favorite. I know you hate wearing mascara. I know that for some reason you used to wear baggy boring clothes and all of a sudden this week you've started dressing in color, in clothes that show off an incredible body. And I know that I've wanted to kiss you since the first day I met you. I think you're incredibly hot and sexy and I didn't want you to go home with some random guy tonight. I wanted you to go home with me."

He lowered his head and finally took her mouth against his, kissing her, wrapping her up close. She molded herself to him, full curves pressed against his body, setting him on fire. He knew that kissing Gwen would be pretty awesome, but he hadn't expected just how good. She fit against him like no other woman had ever. She kissed him back, making little sounds that were driving him insane, and he knew that this wasn't going to be enough.

• • •

So, the Muffin Man knew how to kiss.

He kissed her like she was the last woman on earth, like he'd been starved for her. She dug her nails into some pretty fine biceps and whimpered as her knees were about to surrender. He backed her up against the wall, supporting her with his strong body and proceeded to kiss her until she didn't remember where she was.

She screamed and he jumped at the loud pounding on the front door. He swore under his breath and they both turned to see Chase and her brother standing there. Chase was holding a flashlight and Jack looked ready to murder TMM.

"Omigod, hold on," she said, wiping her mouth and straightening out her clothes. Of all the stupid, humiliating things to happen to her. "It's my sort-of-brother-in-law and my brother." She whipped the door open and they came bounding in.

"Why is that guy groping you?" Jack asked pointing at TMM. Chase was aiming the flashlight beam at TMM's face and this whole thing was beginning to look like a police interrogation.

"He's not groping me," Gwen said, looking over at TMM...it did occur to her at that moment that she still didn't know his name.

TMM shot her a look but didn't argue. As TMM walked over to join them, her brother's eyes widened.

"I know you. You're Doctor Thomson, right?" Jack extended his hand and looked like a normal person again instead of barbarian.

She breathed a sigh of relief when TMM took it. Doctor? Huh. So...*not* woodsman.

TMM smiled and nodded. "Right. How are you? How's... Lily?"

Oh, no. Whenever someone asked Jack about Lily he went on for at least half an hour.

"She's fine," she interrupted. "What are you two doing here?" she asked. Leave it to the men in her family to ruin her one night of...whatever it was.

"We were at The Roadhouse when the power went out and knew you were in town so thought we'd check in on you," Chase said.

"Oh, well, thanks, but I'm fine."

"Clearly," Chase said with a cough that looked like he was hiding a smile.

Jack's eyes narrowed on…Dr. Thomson. She really needed to find out his first name, but she couldn't ask now because that would mean Chase and Jack would know she didn't know the name of the man that had been "groping" her. She didn't think referring to him as doctor would do much for her credibility either.

"So you and my sister know each other?"

Gwen kept trying to usher them to the door but they both stood there like trees. She shot TMM a nervous glance. "He's been coming here every morning."

Jack snapped his finger and pointed at TMM. "Oh. The Muffin Man."

She was going to kill her brother. There were many times in her life, growing up with Jack that she'd envisioned herself strangling him, but now, the feeling was so intense that she was forced to clasp her hands together. Just the fact that Jack knew her nickname for him would imply that she'd been so infatuated by him that the entire family knew.

Doctor TMM rubbed the back of his neck. "Luke. My name is Luke."

Oh. Luke. That was a nice name. She eyed him. Yes, it suited him. Luke the Doctor. Very hot. Much hotter than the Muffin Man/Woodsman.

"Well, I guess now that we know you're…safe, we'd better get going," Chase said, backing up a step.

Jack stood still. "Roads are open by the way, so, uh, Luke, you can go home."

"Jack," she said.

He held up his hands and backed up a step. "Right. So we'll see you around, Luke."

Luke gave her another look, but she just threw him her sweetest smile.

"So she managed to snag the Muffin Man," her brother said to Chase before the door had closed all the way.

"Well, good-bye, drive carefully!" she yelled, shutting the door on her brother's face and not waiting for his reply.

She turned her back to the door, raised her arm behind her back, and gave her brother the finger. She heard Chase's bark of laughter and after a few seconds looked over her shoulder to see them walking away. "So, you're a doctor."

He ran a hand over her chin and her body tingled remembering the feel of his stubble against her face. Oh, her brother ruined everything.

"Yeah. ER. Usually I work nights and on my way home in the morning I stop by here."

"Oh…so that's why you always look tired."

"Yeah."

"So, you're the doctor who was there when Lily and Jack came into the ER?"

He nodded, but didn't say anything. She noticed his jaw was clenched and he shifted his gaze from hers. Maybe he didn't like accolades. But what did this mean for them now? Luke had said he was attracted to her, but now it seemed like all the sizzle had followed her brother out the door.

He ran a hand over his jaw and she tingled remembering what that had felt like against her skin. "Gwen."

"Yes," she said clasping her hands in front of her. It always looked like he had a thousand thoughts but never articulated them. It was like he was always in some kind of struggle. She crossed her arms and his gaze dropped to her chest then back up to her eyes. They had that look in them again, the one before he'd kissed her. The one that made her knees feel like they were too jiggly to keep her standing.

"It's not that it didn't mean anything to me, it's just that it doesn't matter because this can't go anywhere."

"Because…"

He dug his hands into his pockets. TMM—Luke, wore jeans like no man she'd ever met. "Because we can't."

Her eyes narrowed on him, realizing he was looking guilty. "Do you have a wife?"

He sighed and looked down. "Widower."

A pang shot through her. That was why he looked so sad all the time. "Oh, I'm so sorry to hear that," she whispered. His jaw was still clenched and his eyes were filled with a pain that made her ache.

He looked down for a moment. "Thanks. It's been a long time."

"Oh." She needed another word. So much about him made sense now.

"Gwen, I'm not in Shadow Creek for long. Just six more months and then I move hospitals. I'm only here temporarily. I don't want...happily ever after anymore. I don't want marriage again."

"Oh," she said, looking down at her boots. She couldn't blame him. "So it would be stupid for us to get involved."

"Exactly."

"Because you're worried that if you get involved with me, I'll fall in love with you and then you'll break my heart because you're a career-oriented doctor who will be able to leave without looking back while I sit here and stuff muffins into my mouth and relive our sordid affair, wishing you were still here?"

He grinned and took a step into her. "Sort of."

"You can't step closer to me, smile like that, and then still plan on leaving."

He shrugged. "So what if I stay...for the evening?"

She looked around. "Here?"

He gave her a nod. "Let's do the speed dating thing you had set up."

Her heart was pounding faster than the day she'd had

two large coffees in a row followed by the dark chocolate muffin and a shop full of customers that needed to be served. She looked around the room. The tea lights were lit, the questions were still lying on the counter…all she had to do was remember what he'd said. He wasn't staying. He wasn't looking for a lasting, committed relationship anymore.

She glanced back at him. He was standing there, his thick dark hair mussed up from her fingers, his stubble all stubbly and appealing, that mouth…she could sacrifice herself. "Okay. I think I'd rather sit on the floor than at the table though."

"Agreed. Do you have any food?"

"I have chocolate. Chocolate muffins and maybe a chocolate chip cookie left."

He grinned, his eyes sparkling. She liked that twinkle. "How about all of the above?"

She laughed. "Fine. I'll put together a small tray of something."

"Great. I'll get an area set up for us to sit."

They both walked in opposite directions and Gwen scrambled to gather the leftovers she had while her mind was racing. She couldn't believe this was happing. TMM, no, Luke, was here. Just the two of them. Sure, he'd basically said he would only be her date out of pity, but she was an optimist. She was going to have to process the fact that he'd been married and lost his wife. It made her feel so bad for him, yet it explained so much. She also knew that it must be a part of the reason he wouldn't get involved with anyone else. It had taken her sister-in-law five years to move on after Michael had died. She wasn't going to think of all this. She was just going to enjoy the moment.

A few minutes later she joined him close to the window. He'd laid out their jackets and taken two of the red pillows they used on the decorative chair in the display corner. The tea lights were surrounding them and it looked cozy and intimate. He took the tray from her and waited while she sat down first and then joined her. He was close enough that she could reach out and touch him, close enough that she felt safe next to his large body.

"Are you eating?" he asked, eyeing the tray.

She smiled. "Go ahead and help yourself. I've had enough chocolate today."

He grabbed a muffin. "Thanks."

"I'm starting the questions," she said, stretching out her legs and crossing her ankles in front of her. He made a noise beside her and she looked over at him.

"I like the boots," he said, his voice thick. A shiver swam through her. "Keep talking. I'm not going to look at the boots."

She skimmed the first few questions trying to ignore the erratic beating of her heart. She wasn't sure she was prepared for TMM and this sexy side of him. She could barely handle his appeal when he grunted out hellos and good-byes. "I already know your name, your job, that you're um…" She coughed. "A widower…okay how about this. Do you believe in love at first sight?"

He frowned and stopped chewing. "I believe in lust at first sight."

She frowned. "Oh, does that happen often?"

He gave a low laugh and leaned his head back against the wall. "No."

She wondered about his wife, but that felt too personal to ask. He didn't seem the type to want to volunteer his feelings.

"But with you, yes."

Oh. *Oh.* That was supposed to be flattering…and flirting. "Thanks. Okay…moving on."

"Wait. I get to ask you the same question, don't I?"

She crossed her arms and looked at him. Good grief, he was beautiful. She liked his rugged looks. She liked the stubble, the messed up hair. She also liked his mouth, she noticed. "I guess, yes. You're right."

"All right, so, do you believe in love at first sight?" Her mouth went dry. His gorgeous face very close to hers, blue eyes twinkling, sensual mouth turned up in a half smile.

She swallowed. "Yes. I believe in love at first sight."

He shook his head and she wondered how she'd never spotted the arrogance until now. "You're mixing them up."

"Uh, I know what I'm doing and I know what I'm thinking. I believe in love at first sight and I'm sticking to that."

"You can't fall in love with someone without knowing them. You can be attracted to them. Those are two different things."

"But what if it turns into love?"

"Well, that's not at first sight."

She pursed her lips. "You're kinda starting to piss me off so let's move on to the next question."

He threw back his head and laughed. She smiled at the sound and the picture he made. "Okay, what's the next one?" She paused as she read it. She didn't know if it was the right question to ask now that she knew about his past.

"We can skip it," she said, quickly scanning the page for the next one.

He snatched the page from her. His jaw clenched for a moment then he asked the question. "What do you look for in a husband or wife?"

"You can go first," she said.

"I'm not sure about husband."

She snatched the paper back. "Seriously."

He shrugged. "Since I have no intention of getting married again, I haven't given it much thought."

Maybe she should let up with the questions. She was pushing too hard. Clearly, he wasn't one to divulge personal details, not that she could blame him. This entire thing wasn't fun and playful given what he'd been through.

"Fine. Honesty. Integrity. Sense of humor. I don't know," he said with a rough sigh, putting down his muffin.

Warmth spread through her at his attempt to play along. It had to mean something, that he would sit here and do this with her. "Okay, I'll go. He has to have a job."

A corner of his mouth turned up. "That's a good one."

"He has to like food, he has to be able to make me laugh, and he has to be loyal. No guy with a wandering eye. I can't stand that."

"Agreed."

"Oh, and smart. I can't be married to someone stupid, because I might take advantage of them."

She had to stop speaking because now he was howling, holding his stomach and laughing. She poked him in a very well defined shoulder and waited for him to calm down. He slowly stopped laughing and looked at her in a way that made her toes curl and her breath catch. "We can't be doing this."

She smoothed out her hair. "Right. Back to the questions. Do you want kids?"

He frowned but didn't say anything for what had to be at least a minute. "No."

Her heart sank. What was she doing? He had the opposite answers than she did on basically everything. How could she be falling for a guy that didn't want marriage or children? They sat there, neither of them saying anything. She glanced out the large window, the snow had slowed enough that now it looked like it was meandering gently from the sky.

"Do you?" he asked, breaking the silence. His voice was thick, filled with emotion.

She drew her gaze from the window to him. "Yes."

He gave a nod and then picked up his discarded muffin. "Huh."

She glanced down at the sheet of questions again, suddenly desperate to push this conversation along. Things weren't looking good. "Moving along… Do you like animals? Do you have a pet?"

"No. I like dogs though. No time and I haven't been in the same place long enough to have one."

She was thrilled. He liked dogs? That was very promising.

He stopped chewing. "Why are you smiling at me like that?"

She lifted the paper to cover her face and smile. "No reason."

He plucked the paper from her hand. "Do you like animals?"

She smiled and nodded. "We adopted a dog. Lola. It was when my dad was going through cancer treatments. Our house was pretty empty at that point and things were bad. I thought that a dog might bring us some joy and cheering up, and she did."

He was looking at her intently. "You've had a rough few years."

She nodded. She hadn't wanted to get into this part of her life, because this was the part that hurt the most. Shadow Creek was a small town so she'd never had to tell anyone what had happened and that was easier. Telling someone she barely knew about the darkest days in her family history was disconcerting.

"You don't have to tell me, Gwen."

"A little over five years ago my brother, who was Jack's twin, was in an awful car accident. He had his son in the car and they both died," she said, her voice trailing to a whisper. Sometimes it felt as though time had gone so fast, that it all seemed so long ago. Sometimes she didn't think about Michael and Matthew for a few hours and the world seemed just as it should. But then she'd remember and that hole that she always thought could somehow be filled again, stung again with emptiness.

"Everything fell apart then. We all fell apart. Jack left town, left Lily behind and broke her heart. My sister-in-law Julia left town because she couldn't cope with her loss either. It was me and my parents…and Chase and his little girl Maggie. They aren't related to us—well, now that he and Julia are married, I guess in a roundabout way they are. But they were always family."

"I'm so, so, sorry."

She whipped her head in his direction because the emotion in his voice was so blatant and was touched to see tears in his eyes, his features tight. "Thank you."

He ducked his head. "It must have been awful."

"It was the hardest time in my life. There were so many days that I was just angry. Angry that Jack took off and left me with our parents. Angry that I was so alone. Lily disappeared into herself, not wanting to be around anyone. Julia was gone. I mean, everyone was gone. Chase and I were there and that was it. But I watched my parents age that year and I swear I thought they were going to die too."

His jaw was clenching and unclenching.

"Sorry, I guess this isn't really the best topic to be discussing when you barely know someone, right?"

He shook his head, looking down still. "This is part of who you are. You're a very strong person, Gwen. I'm sure your parents wouldn't have gotten through it without you."

She shrugged. "We are a very close family and I know that they would do anything for me too. I guess we can all say we came out on the other side though. We figured out how to live without two people we loved. Jack and Lily are having twins. Chase and Julia are married. Everyone is happy again," she whispered.

"What about you?" he asked, this time turning to look at her. She couldn't quite figure out his expression. His eyes looked as though they were filled with pain…and something else.

"Me? I'm…fine. I'm happy I have my business now with Lily. I'm happy we're all in Shadow Creek and living our lives together."

"No men? Firefighters?"

She groaned. "I haven't had time for guys. I haven't had time for a life, really. I lived with my parents and that was my entire life. I feel like now I'm finally getting back on track and I'm happy I've moved out and have some breathing space. Ben and I are friends. Also, I can be slightly picky when it comes to men."

"So I should be flattered?" he asked with an adorable grin.

She punched him in the shoulder. "You should be very flattered. You passed all my tests."

His smile faltered for a second and the mood shifted. Him telling her about his wife reminded her that he wasn't just the average single guy. He had lost a spouse. "Luke, I know that you don't want a relationship. You're not going to break my heart. Thank you for telling me about your wife."

The lights flickered a few times and then turned back on. Blue headlights, rumbling, and then the snow plow driving by the front window ended their captivity. Something happened. It was as though TMM went back to just being the guy at the bakery. She felt his detachment even before he hopped to his feet and offered her a hand. "Why don't I help you close up and walk you home?"

She tried to hide her disappointment. What was going on? Hadn't they just shared something special? Hadn't the kiss meant anything for him? She forced a smile and began collecting the votives, blowing them out as she went. "Sure, I'll be a minute." She walked to the back, blinking back her tears as she found her jacket and hat and gloves. She was not going to show him how hurt she was. He had easily ended their evening, he had no problem walking away.

Basically, he'd come here tonight out of pity.

Luke the Doctor believed in lust at first sight and nothing more.

She believed in love at first sight, and now she was going to pay for it.

Chapter Five

Luke was finishing up the night shift and now that he was done working, could focus on Gwen. He hadn't seen her since the other night, and he cursed himself for ever walking into the shop after her speed dating night.

What had he been thinking? He'd been attracted to her the moment he laid eyes on her. He'd known having a conversation with her would be bad, because it would only mean he'd like her even more, which he now did. He'd replayed everything she'd said in his mind, including how she'd said it, the look on her face, and in her eyes.

And him opening up about Lisa. Then there was the kiss. He was so screwed.

If he pretended like it didn't mean anything to him, he'd be a jerk and a liar. If he started something with her, he'd be an even bigger jerk and liar, and he'd end up breaking her heart. No matter what, he'd just made his life and hers way more complicated. He couldn't ignore her.

He didn't want to be married again. He didn't deserve to be married again or a father again. Gwen deserved all those things, but with another man.

He walked through the sliding doors and out into the brisk Montana morning. The cold air felt good against his hot skin and he didn't bother buttoning up his jacket. For the first time since moving here, he was planning on skipping the chocolate shop tomorrow morning. Even though that meant he had nothing to look forward to.

"Dr. Thomson!"

Luke fought the groan in his throat and turned in the direction of the voice. He had almost escaped the hospital. When he was done with his long shift, he always made every attempt at getting out of here as quickly as possible. He didn't want to get too close to anyone, he didn't want any friends. That way when he left no one would know him enough to miss him and vice versa.

He waved at the nurse running toward him. She was friendly and a great asset to the team. "Hi, Wendy."

"I wanted to know if you're coming to the staff party next week. I'm running it so I'm trying to get everyone's numbers." He didn't move when she stepped into him and touched his arm. Crap. He had touched Wendy many times, passing charts, supplies, but in no other way. In fact, he went so out of his way not to encourage anything that he wondered if people thought him socially awkward.

He didn't do staff parties. Or any parties anymore. "Thanks, but my sister is probably coming into town."

"Hi."

He didn't breathe as he heard Gwen's voice beside him.

Wendy dropped her arm, disappointment flashing across her face at Gwen's appearance. Gwen didn't look all too pleased, no doubt incorrectly assuming something was up with him and Wendy. He had no idea why Gwen was even here.

"Well, I'd better get back to work, my break's almost

over," Wendy said with a forlorn sigh. Oh God. There were too many women and feelings to keep track of. "Uh, Gwen this is Wendy. Wendy, this is Gwen. My…friend."

Gwen was beaming at him and he was taken aback by the sight of her so happy. He actually found himself smiling back at her, despite the absurdity of the situation. "Nice to meet you, Wendy."

"You too," Wendy said. She gave a little wave and left.

He turned to Gwen when Wendy was out of earshot. "Hi, what are you doing here?"

She held up a bag and a paper coffee cup. "I thought that since you had to work on a Sunday and the shop is closed I'd bring you a little something."

He shoved his hands in his pockets, hating that she had done this for him. She was impossible to resist. Her cheeks were rosy and her eyes were filled with something that looked like excitement to see him. She had on a furry red hat and her lips were red…and so damn irresistible. Resist, Luke. Resist. He took the bag and coffee. "You didn't have to do that."

She shrugged, looking away. "So…guess I'll be going."

He sighed roughly. "Gwen."

She was currently fiddling with the buttons on the front of her coat. "You don't need to say anything. I know this is where you say you have regrets. The kiss was a mistake."

"No, this is where I say I'm interested as hell and, yeah, the other night was the best damn mistake I ever made. But that still doesn't mean we can go anywhere."

Her mouth had dropped open and it took every ounce of self-control he possessed not to kiss her. "Then why fight it? Why don't we see where things go? In a few weeks we might hate each other and I'll be waving you off as you leave Shadow Creek."

He laughed, except then he remembered she probably would be hating him in a few weeks, just not for the reasons she was implying. "I don't want you to get hurt."

Her gaze darted to the hospital. "Why, because you're the hot doctor everyone wants and you leave a string of broken hearts wherever you go?"

He rubbed the back of his neck torn between wanting to kiss her and regretting ever kissing her in the first place. "No."

"I've spent the last five years ignoring my own needs. The world moved on. People moved on. I stayed the same. But something inside me clicked a couple weeks ago and I'm done letting life pass me by without being who I really am or going after what I really want. I'm not going to waste time throwing myself at a man who doesn't want me."

For a second it looked as though she was about to kick him in the shins, but instead she turned, ready to storm off. He couldn't let that happen. He couldn't let her go.

He grabbed her wrist, tugging her backward until she bumped into his chest. He placed the coffee and muffin on the hood of his car and wrapped his arms around her, kissing her neck from behind. She leaned against him, relaxing. He ignored the warning inside and went instead with the warmth, the happiness, she brought him. She turned around, looking up at him. "Don't play games with me. One minute you want me, the next you don't."

He cringed inwardly at the hurt in her eyes even though her voice was strong. He didn't want to lie to her, he didn't want to pretend he wasn't developing feelings for her, or that he wasn't attracted to her.

"This is not a matter of not wanting you or playing games. I don't play games. I have no interest in games. I'm not the man you want. I'm not the man you need. I will screw up your life if you let me close," he said, feeling the lump in his throat. He hated emotion. He tried not to feel as much as possible, but Gwen brought out all the emotion in him because Gwen was everything he'd been trying to hide from for the last five years.

Those brown eyes of hers looked right through him, forcing him to admit how badly he wanted her. "You can't tell me what or who I need. You can't tell me who I can fall in love with. All I know is that life passes by and if you're too afraid to take a risk, one day it'll be all over and there'll be nothing to show for our time here. If you don't want me, that's one thing. But to not even try because you're afraid? I don't think so."

With that, she turned on her heel and started walking away.

Hell. Well, he'd warned her.

He grabbed her wrist and she paused, then turned around.

"Ah, Gwen," he said, framing her face with his hands, feeling her cold, soft skin beneath his hands. Wind whipped around them, but he wasn't aware of much except that he was sinking further into this place where he was beginning to ignore all the reasons they couldn't get involved. "I always want you. Not one minute goes by where I don't want you," he said, before lowering his head and kissing her.

Gwen wrapped her arms around him and kissed him back with the same passion as the other night, one that matched his. Soon he had her backed up against his car, his body covering hers. He forgot they were in the hospital parking lot until the sound of ambulance sirens in the distance infiltrated his desire-clouded head. He reluctantly stepped back, liking that she still held onto the front of his jacket. Her lips were red and her cheeks were rosy and she looked even more delicious than before.

"I guess I'll see you tomorrow morning?"

He grinned. "Yeah. See you tomorrow," he said, leaning in for another quick kiss.

He'd figure it all out later. There had to be a way to make all of this okay. All he knew was that this woman, somehow, made him feel like the man he wanted to be. She made him feel like there was hope. She made him believe in redemption.

• • •

Luke swung open the door of The Shadow Creek Chocolatiers, desperate to see Gwen's gorgeous face.

He'd had a brutal night at the hospital; they had been short-staffed, the one OBGYN on call hadn't been able to get to the hospital because she was down with the flu so he'd ended up having to deliver a high-risk pregnancy baby and thankfully everything had finally worked out. He hated nights like that at the hospital. He was so damn tired he wasn't even planning on his run when he got home. He just wanted to see Gwen's smiling face, hear her laugh with customers, and then he'd go home and sleep.

He still hadn't figured out what he was going to do, but the uncomfortable feeling that he was going to cross the line with her was approaching. He was going to have to tell her soon or he was going to have to distance himself. He had a few months left on his contract and then he was free to leave Shadow Creek. He wanted to be able to tell them and then leave.

The stupid, childish part of him wished that he could tell her and that she'd forgive him. But Gwen wasn't behind the counter; it was her sister-in-law, Lily.

"Good morning!" Lily called out when he walked in. He hadn't known that night of the blizzard when Jack had walked into his ER with Lily in his arms, who they were. He didn't look at Jack's last name until both of them had been stabilized. And then it had clicked. He'd been worried they'd know who he was, but luckily he had a common last name and no one thought twice about it.

She inhaled sharply as he approached the counter,

clutching her chest. "Dr. Thomson!"

He smiled at her and approached the counter. "You can call me The Muffin Man."

She burst out laughing. "That's okay. I heard you have a real name."

He grinned. "Yeah. Luke."

"Right."

"You're looking well. Feeling good?"

She nodded, still smiling. "I feel great."

"Good, good. Where is Gwen this morning?"

Lily scrunched up her nose and began filling his order that apparently everyone already knew. She placed a steaming cup of coffee on the counter. "She came down with the flu and is refusing all help from us. She doesn't want me to go to her place because I'm pregnant. She doesn't want Jack to go in case he picks it up and gives it to me. Her parents are on a cruise. And she doesn't want Julia to go in case she's pregnant too."

He wasn't the type to worry, normally, but Gwen was different. "Can I get my order to go?"

She nodded and began packing everything up. "Are you going to see her?"

He nodded. "Yeah, the strain that's going around right now is pretty bad. We admitted five patients last night due to complications."

Her brow furrowed. "I was going to drop some food off after work tonight."

"Don't worry about it. I'll check in on her," he said, dropping a bill on the counter and grabbing his coffee cup and paper bag with the muffin. He walked toward the door and gave her a wave over his shoulder. He jogged down the street and up the flight of stairs to Gwen's apartment after getting directions from Lily.

He knocked on the door loudly and waited for an answer.

He knocked again and called her name through the door. Still no answer. He tried the door but it was locked. This time he banged on the door and thankfully he heard slow footsteps. A moment later she opened the door a crack but before he could get a word out, yelped and shut it in his face.

"Gwen, open the damn door."

He heard a thump and he assumed it was her head against the door. "You can't see me like this. I'm dying."

"Open the door because I can bet you you're going to pass out if you keep standing."

When he didn't hear anything after a minute he slowly opened the door, sliding her along the floor since she'd been sitting behind it. He put his things down on the counter and crouched down in front of her. "God, you look like hell."

She attempted to shove him but missed. Her eyes were glassy and her face was grey. Her hair was a tangled heap around her and her lips were parched. "I'm going to help you back into bed."

She moaned and slid over into a fetal position on the ground. "I will never forgive you for this," she mumbled. Her voice sounded hoarse. "Leave me to die with my dignity."

"Do you have ibuprofen?"

She nodded against the floor.

"Have you taken any?"

"Too tired."

"Okay, tell me where it is."

"Bathroom."

He stood and walked around, finding the bathroom quickly in the small apartment. He found the medicine cabinet, grabbed the Advil and then filled up a glass with water and walked back over to her. She was snoring on the ground. "Gwen, wake up," he said, rubbing her back. She didn't move except the shallow rise and fall of her chest. Her skin was boiling under his hand, but she was dressed like she was ready for a blizzard. He needed to get her temperature down.

"Gwen, you have to sit up, okay? I'm going to give you some Advil and water."

"Go away, TMM," she mumbled.

He smiled and managed to get her into a sitting position, leaning her back against the door. She was frowning at him through barely opened eyes. He held the Advil in front of her lips and she finally opened her mouth and he placed the cold water at her mouth, holding the glass so she could sip it. She sighed after swallowing and leaned her head back against the door. "You should go," she croaked. "Save yourself from this plague."

"I never get sick," he said, moving the glass of water and Advil aside. "I've been exposed to all of this anyway. If I was going to get it, I'd already have gotten it."

"I never get sick, either, and look at me now, on death's door with a Muffin Man who doesn't want a committed relationship here at my side. What kind of gruesome hell has my life become?"

He laughed despite himself. "We'll talk about the gruesome hell your life is after you're feeling better. Let's get you to bed. I'm also going to take these layers of clothes off. You have a raging fever and you're bundled up like it's a damn blizzard in here."

"You're not taking clothes off me. I'm freezing."

He eyed what would be the safest article of clothing to take off. She was wearing four layers of socks. "Socks are coming off, Gwen," he said, not waiting for her reply. She actually looked like she was sleeping again. He pulled off her socks and she barely moved. He frowned, sitting back on his heels. Her bathrobe was a furnace of fleece. "Gwen, I'm taking off your robe." He undid the pink belt loop and her hand came down on his.

"No."

"I'm a doctor. Don't be embarrassed. I'm going to get this off you and then get you to bed."

She muttered something that didn't sound very polite but dropped her hand. He opened the belt and pulled the robe down her shoulders and pulled her arms out of the fuzzy robe. She was wearing a clingy tank with spaghetti straps and no bra. He shut his eyes for a second and turned away. He reminded himself he was a doctor. But Gwen wasn't his patient, and she was also a woman to whom he was incredibly attracted. None of that mattered, he told himself as he tried to help her into a standing position, because she was practically unconscious and that would make him a perv for checking her out.

She leaned heavily on him and they slowly made their way to her bedroom. "Okay, sit on the edge of the bed and I'm going to fix this up for you," he said, making sure she wasn't going to fall off before he stripped the bed of the five layers of blankets. He fluffed up the pillows, straightened out the sheets, and then helped her in.

"Why are you here?" she asked. He tried to focus on what she was saying but she was distracting him with her incredible body as her breasts looked ready to spill out of the top of her tank that left nothing to his imagination. He feebly attempted to pull it up but that only ended up leaving her smooth stomach bare. His mouth was dry. He quickly pulled up the sheet and tucked it under her chin.

"I'm so cold. What kind of sadistic doctor takes away a patient's blankets?"

That was more like it. "You had too many and you have a fever. I'll give you one blanket," he said, looking for the thinnest one. "That ibuprofen should kick in and should help regulate your temperature in a bit." He noticed there was no water glass on her nightstand. "Besides the water I just gave you, have you had anything to drink lately?"

She shook her head. "Not since...I have no idea. All I know is that yesterday afternoon I was feeling okay and then by dinnertime it was like I had a plague and haven't moved since."

Classic flu. "Okay. I'm going to keep giving you water and some immune boosting supplements, okay? You need to sleep and be a good patient." He couldn't resist adding that last bit in because he knew it would bother her.

Sure enough, she attempted opening her eyes but instead of making a sassy comeback, her eyes filled with tears and she whispered, "Thank you."

His throat constricted at the unexpected emotion that coursed through him. He leaned down and brushed the hair off her face. "Just rest, okay?"

She was already asleep. He stood there for a moment, knowing he was falling deeper into this abyss Gwen was creating. She was the woman he was supposed to stay away from. She was part of the family that he needed to repay. It was becoming harder and harder to walk away from her, but he knew that he shouldn't worry about that.

As soon as she found out who he really was, she'd walk away from him.

• • •

Gwen opened her eyes, feeling as though a deep fog was finally lifting. She was disoriented but then recognized her bedroom. She was lying in bed. She had the flu, that's what she remembered...panic flooded her exhausted system and she lay there perfectly still as groggy memories of her very hot Dr. TMM scorched her. Was he still here? She turned her head slowly to the direction of her door; it was open.

"Yeah, it's Dr. Thomson."

He was still here! His deep voice, slightly hushed, could

be heard from her bedroom. She listened to see if she could make out what he was saying. It sounded like he was on the phone.

"I should be able to get back to work tomorrow." There was a pause. How much time had he taken off work? For her? "Ah, I'll remind you, Noreen, I haven't taken off a single day since I've been here and I've covered way more shifts than anyone else." He spoke in an authoritative voice even though he was still being polite to "Noreen." A moment later she heard him say that he'd see her tomorrow and then she heard him walking around. Was he coming in her direction? She tried to lift her arms to check her hair but it took way too much effort because it felt as though her arms weighed one hundred pounds each.

Seconds later, he was standing in her doorway looking like every dream she'd ever had about him. His hair was damp, which meant he'd showered in her shower. His hands were bracing either side of the door and his T-shirt was hugging some pretty hot muscles and chest. He was wearing some worn and scruffy jeans that matched his stubble. And she… well, she was a hideous creature she was pretty sure. Except he wasn't looking at her like she was all that hideous. His blue eyes were all soft and there was concern in his face.

"Hey, you're awake. How are you feeling?"

"Kind of like hell, but not as bad a hell as the last few days," she said, wincing as she heard how hoarse her voice sounded.

"Do you think you can sit up and drink water?"

A wave of memories flooded her—him holding a glass of water to her head, giving her medication, tucking her in, smiling at her, brushing hair off her face…omigod. She nodded, trying to slowly get up even though her muscles ached. She managed to drink the water. "How long have I been out?"

"I've been here for three days, but you got sick the day before that. So, you're on day five of the flu."

Her eyes widened. He had been here for three days? She moaned. "Omigod, I'm so sorry. Please don't tell me you've been here that long. You didn't need to stay here. I would have been fine."

"It was no big deal. You were a great patient," he said with a grin that suggested otherwise.

"I think I want to go take a shower," she said, feeling gross and now self-conscious with Mr. Hot Doctor/TMM standing there looking all gorgeous and…clean.

"I can help," he said with a grin that made her heart skip a few beats.

"As if."

His grin widened for a moment, those blue eyes twinkling. "Okay, but in all seriousness, I don't think you should rush out of bed yet. You haven't walked or had a solid meal in days. You'll probably be dizzy."

She sat up a little straighter and slowly brought her legs around the side of the bed. She heard him cross the room and he sat beside her on the bed. She couldn't believe he'd been here for days. He barely knew her. They kissed once. No, twice. But he'd taken time off work. He'd slept here. He'd seen her at her worst. She really needed a shower. "I think I'll make it to the shower."

He gave her a nod. "Okay. Just yell if you need me."

She was not going to blush; she was just going to walk out of the room. Except walking wasn't as easy as she thought it would be. She made it around the bed and then sat down again. "What's wrong with me?"

"It's what's wrong with the entire population in the winter that gets influenza. It can suck the life out of you for weeks. You've actually gotten through it pretty quickly."

"Thanks to you, I guess. Not everyone has a doctor

waiting on them hand and foot."

"Ah, you just needed rest and fluids. I barely did a thing."

That wasn't true, but she wasn't ready to deal with that until she felt somewhat human again. "Okay, I'm going to do this." She eyed the bathroom down the hallway as she looked out the door. She could totally make it there, which led her to another round of memories…omigod going to the bathroom. She whipped her head in his direction.

He held up a hand and grinned. "I helped you to the bathroom and then shut the door. Relax. It's nothing I haven't seen before."

She glared at him. "Your bedside manner is really lacking. I can barely remember anything," she said.

The teasing smile left his face and he looked at her with such tenderness that she wanted to sigh out loud. "You had a nasty fever. Listen, nothing to be embarrassed about. You wouldn't believe the stuff I see," he said, shooting her a reassuring smile.

Great. What a wonderful way to attract a man. He was now comparing her to the horrors he'd witnessed in the ER. "Thanks. I think I can make it there on my own," she said, forcing her legs to work. She stood and didn't move for a moment, careful to be sure all her clothes were actually on. God only knows what he'd seen these last few days. She tried lifting her feet but ended up shuffling her way to the bathroom. She breathed a sigh of relief and braced her arms on the counter.

"You okay?" he asked.

"Yup. I'm shutting the door now…taking a shower." She shut the door but didn't lock it, just in case. She managed to brush her teeth while at the same time doing an examination of her sorry looking face. She looked like hell. She grabbed one of her folded and fresh towels from the cupboard and hung it on the hooks beside the shower—next to the other damp towel. His. Right. Because Luke had stayed here and showered here. She turned on the water and let it warm up, worried because she'd barely done anything and now her energy was almost gone. She needed to shave too, she realized as she looked down at her legs. Moaning she climbed into the shower.

After finally finishing everything and feeling human, if not exhausted, she toweled herself off. Blow drying her hair was out of the question because that required way too much energy. She could brush it out and after looking at herself in the mirror, she could finally say she looked respectable again. She realized she had no clothes. All she had was the towel she was wearing. So, she had a few options—she could ask him to give her clothes but that would mean him rummaging through her underwear drawer, or she would have to walk across the apartment in only a towel. Well…she had shaved. Towel it was.

She tiptoed out of the room, happy she didn't see him in the kitchen or TV area. She stopped in her doorway at the sight of him. He'd changed sheets, the old ones in a heap in the corner. The windows were slightly open, a cool, but welcome breeze coming through. The bed was freshly made, there was ice water on her nightstand, and everything looked so welcoming. Tears stung the back of her eyes—until she saw him looking at her. His eyes weren't looking very sorry for her anymore. Instead, they had that glint they'd had the night they kissed. She curled her toes into the hardwood floor and searched for something to break the awkwardness.

"You didn't have to do all this," she said, clutching the towel in one hand and pointing to her bed with the other.

He shrugged. "You'll feel better now that you've showered and have a fresh bed."

"I, um, forgot clothes."

He grinned. "I wasn't complaining."

She felt her face heat up.

"Why don't I get you something to eat while you get dressed and back into bed?"

She nodded. "Um, okay. You don't have to do anymore. I'm fine now," she said. She realized she didn't want him to leave. She had been comforted by his presence and maybe that's how she'd been able to rest without worry.

He walked past her, pausing to kiss the top of her head. "I'll be right back."

She was speechless. She worked as fast as she could at finding something to wear that wasn't frumpy or sexy. It was a difficult task. She wasn't going to even attempt the torture of a bra, she'd just hide under the covers. Besides, God only knew how many times she must have flashed him. She tried not to groan out loud at the embarrassment of it all. She quickly dressed, settling on pink plaid pajama pants and a T-shirt. She shrugged into a hoodie as he walked back into the room.

"So I have some more bone broth for you and a banana."

Who was this guy? "What's bone broth?"

"You've been sipping it all week. It's like chicken stock but better. It's really good for you, rich in minerals and has compounds that boost the immune system and are soothing to the gut," he said, walking across the room to place it on her nightstand. Great. Guts. Clearly, he was now just thinking of her as a patient, because you couldn't go from barely dating to seeing a person at their worst and having conversations about guts then move back to romance. He stood there looking at her, his hands in those amazing jeans of his, wide shoulders slightly hunched.

"You look much better," he said, with a slight smile.

"I can't believe you did all this, and honestly, I have no idea what to say. I'm embarrassed and appreciative all at the same time. I guess free coffee and muffins for you for the rest of your life."

He laughed that rich, deep laugh that always made her smile and her toes curl and her stomach flip around a few times. He was the most handsome man she'd ever met, but he was caring too. He filled up her small bedroom, and when his laughter stopped and they stared at each other a bit too long, he ran his hands through his hair. "So, uh, I guess I'll be going."

Panic filled her. She didn't want him to leave. She wanted him here. He started walking toward the door. "Wait," she said, not knowing what she was going to say. *Quick, think of something.* "I don't feel like sleeping yet. I was thinking of watching TV."

He gave a nod, his eyes not revealing anything.

"Do you…I mean, I know you're probably dying to go home and I've already wasted so much of your time."

"You didn't waste my time, Gwen. If I didn't want to be here with you, I wouldn't have been."

She swallowed. Oh. "Um, thanks. Do you want to stay a bit and watch TV with me?"

His gaze went from her to the door and she had the sinking feeling he was going to leave. This would be the end of her sordid affair with TMM. She had scared him off with her disgusting flu.

"You know what? Never mind," she said, trying to look casual. "It's okay. I know—"

"Sure," he said.

She eyed the bed. The fresh sheets and nicely made covers beckoned and the thought of climbing in there was becoming more appealing by the second, especially if Luke was joining her. She settled into her side and he rounded the corner to the other side. She fiddled around with the covers while he stretched out beside her, but on top of the covers.

"You find something to watch," she said, handing him the remote while she picked up the oversized mug of broth. The air felt thick as they sat side by side on the bed. She resisted the urge to rest her head on his shoulder or, better yet, curl up against his warm body. She sipped the warm, soothing broth while he flipped through the channels. "Sorry, basic cable," she said when the first round of channels turned up nothing appealing.

"That's okay. I haven't watched TV in months."

"Really?"

He shrugged. "No time."

"What did you do here for the last three days?"

"Reading. Medical charts. I was able to catch up on a lot of stuff."

His work ethic was admirable and made him even more attractive, if that was even possible at this point. She finished off the broth and then drank half the glass of water. "That was good. Did you make it?"

He turned a little to her and he was so close that she could see the darker blue flecks of his eyes, the fine lines…and the mouth. She shouldn't look at his mouth. "No. I bought it at the natural food place."

"Still appreciated," she said, turning back to the television. She yawned and snuggled down into the covers a bit more.

"Tired?" he asked, his voice as soothing as the soup.

"It's so sad. I've been sleeping for days."

"Yeah. The flu sucks. Don't expect to be fully back to normal for at least another week."

She groaned. "I have so much to do. Poor Lily must be wiped."

"She's fine, don't worry. You'll be able to get back to work, you're just going to be dragging for a bit."

If he would lie down beside her, she didn't even think she'd resist reaching out for him. He was like this big, hot, protector and she didn't even care what that meant about her. There was something about having him around that reminded her of how lonely she'd been. He adjusted his pillow and then lay down beside her, one arm tucked under his head. She let her gaze roam for a few seconds, taking in the hard length of his body, the way his flat stomach dipped and then his hard chest rose and fell with each breath. Then up to that great jawline, the sensual mouth, and the eyes…that were staring at her. "Gwen, I swear to God, stop checking me out."

"Ah!" she yelped. "I was not!"

His chest rumbled. "You were. Just like I'm checking you out. We can't do that. Remember, we can't get involved with each other." His voice lit up every nerve ending in her body and she wanted to cry or curl into him. "Besides," he continued in that deep, husky voice, "you're still weak. Sick. We can't do anything that would require physical exertion."

• • •

He'd always been a sucker for punishment. But being here, with Gwen looking all soft and sweet beside him in her bed, made him forget all the reasons they couldn't be together.

There had been many days after the accident that he wished he wasn't alive. Guilt kept him from living. He had so many damn regrets. So many regrets about Lisa, about their baby. Things he'd never share with anyone. After the accident he had no interest in women, in relationships, in happily ever afters.

Gwen was the queen of happily ever after. She screamed of promises of forever and love. She believed in all of it. He had none of that left in him. A part of him wished he did. He wished he'd met her when he was younger. He wished he was a different man so that he could act on his feelings toward her. And he felt. A lot.

She brought out many sides to him. She made him remember who he was when he was younger, when his mother was still alive. At one time, he'd been full of hope. Gwen brought out the man in him again, because he was very aware of her on a sexual level. He wanted her. She brought out a side of him that made him want to fall in love. That was dangerous, not acceptable.

"As if I'm suggesting anything," she said, with an adorable disgruntled frown.

He grinned and lay down beside her, knowing this was dangerous territory, but willing to take the risk. "C'mere, Gwen."

She eyed him and he lifted his arm and a second later she was snuggled up against him, her head resting on his shoulder, her soft body pressed against his side, as though they'd lain like this for a lifetime. It felt good. She felt good. It had been a long time since he'd felt this close to a woman. Her damp hair fell against his chest, her hand resting above his stomach. He could feel her breasts rise and fall with each breath he took and he forced himself to concentrate on the television. "I'm not sure I said thank you," she whispered. "But thank you."

He leaned forward to kiss the top of her head. Her index finger was now making little circles on his chest so he grabbed it and flattened it on his chest. "Stop. No physical exertion, remember? You can't get all sweaty."

"Sorry…oh…*oh*. I'd get sweaty?" Her voice was all breathy and she clutched a fistful of his shirt.

His teeth were clenched so hard he had to mentally concentrate on unclenching them. They needed to change the conversation topic. "You should sleep."

"Yes."

"Gwen."

"Yeah?"

"For the record, this is torture. A very hot form of torture, but still torture."

"Good to know," she said, and he smiled at the curl of her

lips against his body. "Speaking of hot, you're like a furnace. I might need to take my sweater off."

"No."

"Yes, really, I think I'm overheating."

"That's not me. You're keeping your sweater on."

She moved and the sound of the zipper was like pure hell as he stared at the ceiling remembering everything he'd done, all the reasons this couldn't happen. She tossed it on the corner of the bed. "There," she said, and snuggled back into him like she'd been doing this for years.

"Fine. Just stop moving for God's sake."

"I'm going to sleep."

How the hell could she sleep? "I'm…never going to sleep again."

She patted his chest and he caught her hand and kissed it. He ignored her soft gasp and then placed her hand back on his chest and covered it with his. "Don't make noises like that either."

"Can I ask you something?"

He stopped smiling when he heard the hesitation in her voice. "I thought you were going to sleep."

"Thoughts. Lots of thoughts. Also, I haven't spoken in days, it's like I have all these bottled up questions and things that need to be said."

He laughed even though he knew she was going to ask him something about his past.

She poked his chest. "Do you want to talk…about what your life was like before you came to Shadow Creek. Speaking of, why did you come to Shadow Creek?"

He stiffened. He couldn't answer that last part. Not now. And he didn't want to talk about the rest of it. It involved thinking about his failure. About the most important role he was ever given in life and failed badly. It involved feelings. All things he hated talking about. He also knew that when he told her everything, she would never look at him the same way. At that point there was no going back and he'd lose her. He didn't want to lose her yet. She made him feel more alive than he had in five years. "Nothing much to say, Gwen."

"Do you want to tell me about your life before?"

He stared up at the ceiling. "It was busy. We worked. A lot. We both liked work."

"Oh."

He laughed, even though there was nothing funny about any of this. "Seriously."

"Does your wife have any family?"

Yeah. Her parents had never forgiven him, not that he blamed them. After the accident they had been devastated that their only daughter and future grandchild were dead. No one understood how he could have withstood that accident without a scratch on him. He didn't think about the accident when he was awake. He would push the thoughts away, but they'd sneak up on him while he was sleeping, a gentle, quiet noose that would slip around his neck until he woke up choking for air.

"You don't have to talk about it. I know it's hard," she whispered.

"It's…I'm not good at talking about stuff like that."

"Oh, or maybe you don't want to talk about it because it's too personal and who am I in the grand scheme of things? Just this poor muffin maker."

He started laughing again and she stopped speaking. So wrong on so many levels. "Yes, the poor muffin maker, that's how I think of you." He craned his neck to see her expression and sure enough it was a frown. He sighed. She was important to him now. "Okay, fine. We were both focused on our careers. We met at a time in our lives where we were lonely I think. For a while it worked. It was nice having someone to come home to, but after a while that's all it was. We barely even spoke some days and that started bothering her before me. The night she died we were fighting."

"Oh, I'm sorry to hear that. How long were you married?"

"Five years."

"Did you guys want kids?"

He shook his head and his gut churned at the truthful answer he gave. "Neither of us did."

"So…you never want kids."

He ran a hand over his jaw. "No."

She didn't say anything for a while. "Are you scared to have kids?"

He swallowed hard. "I hadn't actually thought of that."

"Because sometimes I think I wouldn't ever want kids. I can see how much parents love their kids. I see it in my parents, in Julia and Chase. I felt the smallest piece of that with my nephew too. And then when he died, I witnessed Julia destroyed. My parents too. I mean, it hurt to be around them. I was hurt, but they…it was awful. It makes you wonder why put yourself through the possibility of that kind of pain, you know?"

He had stopped breathing. The emotion he had spent so many years running from crept back in, through Gwen's words, through the sadness he heard in her voice. She had clutched his shirt a little tighter as she spoke, instinctively needing something to hold onto. He needed the same. There had been so many nights he'd needed someone to hold, faith to hold onto. There were so many nights he'd wished he wouldn't wake up the next morning. He didn't know how to answer her question, to tell her that he didn't deserve children; he had no right to be a father.

"Maybe you're right," he said, clearing his throat. He cleared his head of the secret he was keeping from her. "I see a lot in the ER. I've witnessed loss so many times and it guts you every time. That's one thing that doesn't get easier.

It never hurts less. You just try and get better, to do more, to save more lives. That's all there is to do."

"You're one of the good guys."

He didn't say anything, just stared up at the ceiling, wishing he had made different choices.

"Sometimes it feels like I've spent the last five years trying to keep my entire family alive. I've turned into this control freak who thinks everyone's survival is dependent on me. I'm realizing that I haven't been living. I've been fearful."

He craned his neck to look at her. "Of what?"

"That they're all going to go too. My brother and nephew went without warning. Everything in our lives was so perfect, we were all so happy and then they were gone. It makes you think of so many things. Like, I don't know how much longer I have with my parents, but I want to make sure I'm doing everything I can to keep them healthy."

"You can't put that kind of burden on yourself."

"I know, it's just easier said than done. I feel bad for them, for everything they went through. I lost a brother and a nephew. They lost a son and grandson and at their age, it's just harder to come back from. Michael was their rock. He was gone. Jack took off. I needed to be there for them."

"Not many people could do what you did, Gwen."

She put her face in her hands and didn't look like the spunky, free-spirited woman he'd come to know. She looked tired and vulnerable. "I did what I could. I'm not trying to make myself sound like a saint or a martyr. I tried to be there for them. The only thing is that along the way, I think I forgot to have my own life and I think I might be…controlling theirs."

He smiled. He wanted to say that this was the beginning of a new life, the two of them but that would mislead her. He had no idea what they'd think of him when he told them the truth.

"Luke?"

"Yeah?"

"Will you be here tomorrow morning?"

He wanted Gwen so badly. He knew it was physical attraction, but he knew there was so much more here too. That's what scared him. He wasn't supposed to have feelings for her. Feelings were going to complicate everything. He was already in too deep. How the hell were they all going to come out of this unhurt? "I have to work, but I'll be here in the morning."

She nodded against his chest. "I think I'm going to miss you."

His chest constricted at her words. She was roping him in. She was sweet and funny and she wasn't afraid of telling him off. She was perfect. "Yeah, I think I'm going to miss you too."

They didn't say anything and he concentrated on the television and not the woman curled so sweetly against him and all the things he'd rather be doing with her tonight. But if all he could do was hold her, then that was more than enough tonight. After a few minutes, he heard her breath deepen and he knew she'd fallen asleep. What the hell was he going to do? How was he going to leave her? He stayed like that for another half hour, until his heart rate finally slowed and he fell asleep.

It was still dark out, Gwen was still attached to him, when the vibration of his phone woke him. It wasn't even six o'clock in the morning. He frowned at the display. Careful not to disturb Gwen, he slowly untangled himself from her and grabbed his phone, worrying as his sister's picture lit his screen. He closed the bedroom door softly before answering.

"Haley, you okay?"

There was a long pause and his gut clenched when he heard the break in her voice. If there was one person in the world who knew the real him, it was his little sister. "Haley talk to me. You're scaring the crap out of me."

"Luke, I'm leaving him."

He fisted his hand and stared out the window of Gwen's living room window. He'd always hated Haley's husband. Right from day one he could tell he was a misogynistic prick. "Okay, do you need me to get you? I'll come and get you." He didn't know how, but he would. He'd go to hell and back for his little sister.

"No," she said in a small voice. "He's at work. I'm grabbing my things and leaving."

"Haley, did he hurt you? Are you safe to leave?" He could barely ask the question without wanting to smash his fist through the window. He didn't know what he'd do if her husband had touched her in anger. He waited, not breathing, for her answer.

"No, he didn't hurt me," she said in a small voice that made him doubt her answer. He squeezed his eyes shut and leaned his forehead against the cold window. He never should have let her marry him. He should have been more vocal about his concerns, but that all went down when he was dealing with his own hell, his own divorce. Fine big brother he turned out to be.

"I will come and get you. Where are you?"

"No, no. I'm okay. I'm coming to you. Are you still in Montana?"

"Yeah, I'm here. I've got a place, you can stay with me. Just be safe. If you need help, if you need anything, tell me. How about money?"

"I have a stash of money," she whispered. "I'll get to you. I'm driving though. I'm taking my time. Don't worry about me. I'll text you details."

Like he could ever not worry about her. "Be safe, Haley."

"I will. I love you, Luke."

"Love you, Haley."

Dammit. He didn't want her to be going through this. She'd been through enough in her life. He had no idea what condition he'd find her in. He had no idea what she'd been through. Whatever it was, he'd get her through it. It had been just the two of them for so long. Their six year age gap didn't seem like much now that they were adults.

He took a deep breath and hoped to hell that ass hadn't hurt her because if he had, there was no way he'd let him off the hook. He'd hunt him down and make him pay.

He glanced over his shoulder as he heard a noise. Gwen was standing in the doorway, her hair falling around her shoulders, her T-shirt clinging to her.

"Who's Haley?"

Chapter Six

Gwen's heart was racing as she waited for Luke's answer. It might have also been racing because Luke, standing in her apartment in only jeans, scruffy hair, and extra stubble was a little too much to handle. Also the fact that he'd slept in her bed last night and she'd clung to him for dear life.

It registered that he was looking at her strangely. Had he spoken?

"Well?"

"Well…what?"

"I said, Haley is my sister."

"Oh." Relief plummeted through her. Then she remembered that he'd sounded concerned for her. "Is she okay?"

He walked across the room to the kitchen, placing his phone down on the counter, and took the coffee canister out of the cupboard. He looked completely at home in her kitchen as he started a pot. "I don't know. I think she will be okay once she leaves her husband."

She walked over to him and wrapped her arms around

him. He looked so worried for her. A second later his strong arms wrapped around her. "She'll be fine. Is she coming here?"

He cleared his throat and nodded against her head. "Yeah. She's tough, even though she shouldn't have to be anymore."

When he didn't elaborate and neither of them spoke, she became very aware of their bodies. And the fact that his chest was naked and very, very delicious. She was also aware of how hard he felt. Everywhere.

"Gwen?"

"Yes," she squeaked.

"You're going to move away from me and get dressed."

She turned her head so that it rested on his chest now. He smelled so good. "I'm all recovered now."

The pounding on the door caused them both to jump apart. They both looked at each other. Neither were in any condition to answer the door.

"Gwen! It's your mother and father! Open this door."

"Well, that's one way to kill the mood!" she said, running to her bedroom to grab her sweater. He followed her, pulling his own shirt on. What a shame, she thought as she looked at him all covered up.

"I swear to God, you've got the most expressive eyes on the planet," he grumbled.

"This is all your fault," she said as she ran out of the room. "Your 'don't fool around with the flu patient rules' have ruined everything!"

"Gwen!"

Gwen whipped open the front door and her parents barrelled through. "I cannot believe you had the flu and didn't call us! We would have come home early from our trip!"

"Seriously? That's exactly why I didn't call you! As if I'd want you to cut your vacation short to come home and take care of me," she said. "Don't hug me," she said as they attempted to get close. "I don't want you to catch it."

Her father was looking around her kitchen, clearly putting his life on the line in search of food.

"Dad, there's no pie. I was sick, remember?"

His face fell. "Right. Of course, sweetheart."

She watched as their eyes widened. Luke. "Oh, and see I wasn't alone. Luke took great care of me. Mom and Dad, this is Luke Thomson. Luke, these are my parents, Cassy and Edward."

Luke came forward and smiled, shaking their hands. "Nice to meet you."

"He's a doctor," Gwen said. "Actually, he's the doctor who treated Lily and Jack the night of the storm."

Gwen's mother did the sign of the cross and Gwen resisted the urge to smile at the theatrics. "My goodness, you just keep saving my children!"

Luke coughed, an odd look on his face. He was probably mortified. "No, it was nothing really."

His mother made a tsking sound. "No, no. This must have been a horrible week. Our Gwen is a delight, but she's very stubborn. That can't make for a good patient."

Gwen rolled her eyes. "Thanks, Mom."

Luke chuckled. "She didn't protest once. She got a pretty nasty flu, so I don't think she had it in her to argue."

Gwen's mother marched over to the kitchen and started taking coffee mugs out of the cupboard. She was taking over like she was ready to host brunch. "Well, it's still kind of you. Why don't you come over for Sunday dinner? It's the least we can do."

His face got that strange look again. Maybe he didn't want to be around all of them. Too much family. They were rather overbearing. Maybe it was too soon. The man had shut down all her advances. The last thing he wanted to do was spend Sunday night with them too.

"Thank you very much, I, uh, will let you know. I'm

expecting my sister in town this week and I don't know the exact day she'll be arriving."

Her mother busied herself pouring coffees. "Oh, how wonderful. Then next Sunday. She's welcome too, of course! The more the merrier."

Wow, she didn't miss a beat at all.

"Thanks, I'll, uh, let Gwen know. You know I'm sorry to just run out of here, but I need to get back home and get to work later, so I'm going to have to skip the coffee."

Her mother looked heartbroken. "Oh, well that's a shame. But that's okay, we'll get to know each other on Sunday. Thank you again for taking care of our daughter. My goodness how nice of you."

Luke was slowly backing away to her bedroom.

"I'll be right back," she said and followed him.

He was throwing his things in a duffle bag. "I better head out of here."

"They scared you off, didn't they?"

He stood and turned to her and again he had that closed-off expression on his face. "They are great people. It's why you are too."

"Well, there's more of us. You'll meet everyone next Sunday."

She could have sworn she saw a flash of panic across his eyes. "I'll let you know."

She wasn't going to be disappointed. She also wasn't going to analyze this crazy relationship she was now in. So they were both attracted to each other. He obviously cared enough to nurse her back to health, without even being asked to. Yet, she knew he was conflicted about being in a relationship again.

She put her hands on her hips not getting why he was suddenly so cryptic. It did occur to her that she had no idea who he really was, where he was from, or about his family. "So, um, am I going to see you at the shop?"

He gave her a nod and walked out.

• • •

Luke finished his shift at the small rural hospital, and for the first time since he'd arrived in Shadow Creek, missed the city hospital. Here, everyone seemed to care if you had an off day. People also wanted to talk to him. Patients and family members went out of their way to thank him. He supposed that was fine if you planned on making this your permanent home. He didn't.

He shut his car door and sank into the frigid leather seat of his SUV. Normally he'd go to The Chocolatiers, but he thought twice about it today. It was Monday and he knew from Lily that Gwen would be back at work today. Yeah, he wanted to see her more than anything or anyone, but he didn't know what the point would be.

He needed to tell them.

His phone buzzed and he was relieved to see his sister's face. "Hey," he said.

"I should be there next week," she said, her voice sounding calmer than it had the other day. She wanted to make a few stops along the way and visit some different friends. He'd advised against it, but like the rest of the women in his life, she'd ignored his advice.

"Good. Everything okay?"

"I didn't realize how okay until I started driving. I feel free, Luke."

He leaned his head back, knowing he was going to have his hands full in the next few weeks between the Baileys and his sister. He wasn't a guy who liked dealing with emotional crap and that's exactly what would be on his plate shortly. "Good. Has John tried to contact you?"

"No. Not at all, and doesn't that just say it all?"

"You're better off without him."

"I know. You were right about him."

"Doesn't matter. What matters is that you left, you're taking control of your life, and you're on your way to a safe place."

"You're the best, Luke."

"Hardly," he said. "Drive safe and text me updates."

"Love you," she said and hung up.

He put his key in the ignition and blindly drove in the direction of downtown Shadow Creek instead of his home. It looked like the need to see Gwen won out.

He swung the door open, the familiar scent of freshly brewed coffee and baking greeting him like a warm blanket. He paused for a second, taking in the sight of Gwen who was busy doing something behind the counter. Her light brown hair was piled up on her head and she was wearing a clingy knit pale blue sweater and jeans. She looked up and gave him one of her gorgeous smiles. He crossed the shop to the counter. "Morning."

"Good morning."

"You're looking better."

"This is very formal for a guy who has seen me at my worst, changed my sheets, and dragged me off the floor."

He grinned, leaning across the counter, his internal conversation telling him not to get lured in. Clearly his body didn't agree. "I'm trying to be polite."

She tapped her pen against her chin. "That's it? So that's the plan? Be polite and pretend nothing ever happened?"

He sighed and straightened up. "Gwen."

She waved that pen around his face. "That won't work. You walked into my life, hotter than hell, and have lured me in with that kiss and then showed me this other side of you. You took days off work for me and took care of me and now you're like, no way? I don't think so, buddy. Bad timing. This is the year of the new Gwen, where I go after what I want, and I get the guy I want. And I want you."

No one had ever accused him of being a saint. There was only so much a guy could take. He rounded the corner, not taking his eyes off her, watching the way she nervously licked her lips. He framed her face and kissed her. Who had he been trying to fool? There was no way he'd be able to walk away from her. He kissed her until she leaned heavily against the counter, until the bells jingling on the door became way too numerous to ignore, and the whistle jarring them too irritating to ignore.

They pulled apart reluctantly and he was satisfied in a purely male way to see that Gwen looked dazed and flushed and thoroughly content. They both turned to see a lineup of very amused regulars. He helped Gwen serve up some coffees to get through the backup of customers. When everyone had their caffeine and chocolate fix, she turned to him, handing him his usual order.

"So now what?'

He'd find a way to tell her and her family. Now, there was no walking away from this woman without a chance. He didn't deserve her or her family. All he could hope for was their forgiveness and understanding. "I have Saturday night off. Why don't I pick you up and we go out?"

Her eyes lit up but she frowned a second later. "I'd love to, but I promised I'd babysit Maggie for Chase and Julia. He hardly ever gets the night off…wait, why don't you come with me? She goes to sleep at eight. We'd still have a night."

Julia. That was one woman he wanted to avoid. "I don't want to put them in an awkward position. I'm also not good with kids."

"You're a doctor. You have to be good with kids. And it's probably good you meet them before Sunday dinner. Also, did I tell you I like that you're a doctor now that I've gotten used to the fact that you're not a woodsman?"

He coughed. "What's a woodsman?"

"I'm not sure, really, but due to your disheveled appearance, rugged looks, and loner behavior that's what I thought you were."

He reached out to pull her closer, realizing how happy she made him. For the first time in five years, he found himself smiling multiple times a day either with her or thinking about her. She was looking up at him, slightly breathless, and he knew that the chemistry they had wasn't the kind that could be ignored. It wasn't anything like what he had with Lisa and he and Gwen had barely even done anything. This was off-the-charts chemistry, the kind that had him fantasizing about her all the time.

"You can't kiss me here," she said, poking his shoulder and then patting it and smoothing out his jacket. "Seriously, come with me Saturday night."

"Gwen." He didn't want to go to Chase and Julia's house.

"They won't mind. I'll ask first. If I even detect a bit of hesitation, I'll let you know. I guess there is the off chance Chase wants to do a police check on you."

He stopped breathing until she burst out laughing and poked him in the ribs.

"Just joking! Seriously, meet me there at seven. It'll be fun."

"It'll also be PG," he said, thinking that might be for the best.

She flushed. "What exactly were you planning for Saturday night?"

He hadn't planned on Saturday night at all. None of this had been planned, but he couldn't walk away from her and he knew, standing there, that that would be his downfall.

Chapter Seven

"Seriously, it's not a big deal for me to take you to your appointment," Gwen said, shooting her father a look in the rearview mirror.

He was sitting in the back while her mother was beside her in the front seat. How many times had they taken this trip into the cancer center in the city? It had been the three of them for so long but the mood was different now. When her father had first undergone radiation it had been after the accident, while Jack and Julia were gone from their lives. Look at how things had changed for all of them now. Even her. She had Luke in her life now. Never in a million years could she have predicted falling for a man like him—no, actually, she wouldn't have predicted a man like him falling for her. But that was the old Gwen talking. It had taken her way too long to figure out her self-worth wasn't based on her dress size, on her weight loss, or on the way other people perceived her. It was liberating.

She had helped her parents through the darkest times in their family's history and was proud of that, was so grateful for all the people in their lives, and that they were all happy. She had learned to forgive her brother and start over again. The new Gwen was done with comparison.

"Well, we've taken up so much of your time these last few years. You know this is just dad's six month checkup, we could have gone on our own."

Gwen gripped the steering wheel a little tighter, careful not to let her nervousness show. She hated the six-month appointments because they were a reminder of what they'd been through. There was always that small chance that the cancer had returned. She had taken charge when her father had been diagnosed last time—from doctor's appointments, consultations, she had sort of taken over. There was no way she going to leave it to them now. Her mother always had some kind of faith spin on things while her father didn't even seem worried in the least. She wouldn't be surprised if left unsupervised, he'd miss his appointment altogether in search of pie. "Well, I do like hearing what the oncologist has to say and I'd like to be able to ask informed questions if needed."

"Oh, Gwen, have some faith."

"I do. In myself."

"You know, I really don't know how I could have such non-believers for children! I spent your entire formative years instilling God's teachings into you and your brothers."

"Well, I'm sure God also wanted us to use our heads and be prepared if there are…situations that arise that require some thought."

"Everything will be fine, Gwen."

"I'm sure many people have thought the same and then received a devastating diagnosis."

Her father coughed. "Your optimism for my situation is really admirable, dear."

She winced. "Sorry, Dad. I'm sure Mom is right. I just want to hear it for myself."

"Gwen you need to lighten up and not be burdened by us. It's time to concentrate on your own life. What's happening with that handsome doctor? Is he coming over for Sunday dinner?"

Gwen clenched her teeth. Great. Now she had to discuss something she barely knew herself.

"What's his name again?" her father asked.

"Luke."

"He seems like a lovely young man," her mother said. "Quite handsome too."

Oh, yes, he was handsome all right. "Yes, he is. He's nice. Handsome. Hardworking. Caring." She didn't add sexy because that would be gross.

"Does he like pie?"

Gwen sighed, pulling into a vacant parking spot in the packed hospital lot. "I don't know if he likes pie, Dad."

"You should find out."

While Luke's dessert preferences weren't the most pressing concerns she had about him, it did make her very aware of how little she did know about him. Why had he moved to Shadow Creek? It's not like it was an area that was in high demand. She knew his wife had died…but he hadn't told her much else. What about his family? He knew so much about hers. These were all things she was going to find out tomorrow night.

"Dad, I need you to know I can't bake you regular pies anymore."

Her father's eyes widened. "Why?"

She shook her head sympathetically. She understood his disappointment—she shared his love for sweets. "Well, I've seen your blood sugar numbers. I can't be an enabler."

Her father waved a hand. "Never mind these doctors. They're overdramatic."

"Well, judging by the amount of numbers that were in

the red, I don't really think that's what's happening here. But listen, I have been working on a low-sugar, low-carb version of one of your favorite pies. What do you think? I'll bring it over on Sunday."

"No, no, I'm fine. You have enough on your plate, Gwen."

"Meaning you're going to continue eating whatever you'd like."

He laughed. She tried to join in, but she hated that they didn't take their health stuff seriously. It was dangerous. This was why she never should have moved out. Now he could sneak food whenever he wanted.

"Gwen, stop worrying about your father and live your life, dear. We managed to survive up until now."

She wasn't sure how, but she didn't want to start an argument. "Okay, fine. But I will work on some low-carb desserts for you."

He gave her a wink. "No pressure, though."

She smiled. "I'm thinking it might be a nice addition to what we sell at the shop. Maybe a chocolate pecan pie? Or a blueberry?"

His face lit up like Vegas. "I think that's a great idea."

She laughed.

They stepped out into the cold air, walking toward the hospital. She glanced over at her father's profile and her heart squeezed at the tension she saw there. Even though he never let on, she knew he was nervous. She glanced over at her mother, surprised to see the same look on her face. She said a little prayer inside, praying for a clean bill of health for him, praying for some good years ahead, praying for the spring their mother kept insisting they were now in.

• • •

Maggie clapped as she rounded the Monopoly board with her

car. "Yes! I win!"

Gwen and Luke laughed at her enthusiastic outburst. Maggie had warmed up to Luke almost instantly, and Gwen had been surprised by what a natural he was with her. He spent the first few minutes of the night asking her about school and her friends and her special interests. Maggie had loved the attention and had then suggested they play Monopoly together, bragging that she was the family champion. The three of them sat at the dining room table, munching on the veggies and dip and fruit that Chase and Julia had left out for them.

Maggie put a hand on Luke's shoulder. "I think we should play another round. I feel sorry for Luke since he's the new guy. Maybe he needs another shot at winning."

Gwen and Luke burst out laughing.

"It's okay, Maggie, I'm happy you won. You were a tough opponent," Luke said, scruffing the top of her head.

Gwen's ovaries ached just watching him. He was total family man material; he just didn't know it yet. "Yes, Maggie you are an awesome player. But I'm sorry, your parents said that eight is your bedtime, and we're already past that."

Maggie rolled her eyes. "A convenient way to get out of a rematch, I think."

Luke choked on his water and was obviously trying to hide a smile.

Gwen turned to Maggie. She adored the little girl and her spunky nature. "Why don't you get all ready for bed and then call me to tuck you in, okay?"

Maggie nodded, dragging her feet away from the table, while Gwen and Luke started cleaning up the board game and food.

"She's pretty awesome. Really cute," Luke said once they heard her footsteps up the stairs.

"I know, right? She and Chase are considered family.

After…after my brother and nephew died, Chase's wife walked out on him, leaving him to deal with a two-year-old and an intense job. We sort of helped them and took them in, sharing duties with him and helping with Maggie. She went through so much, and had abandonment issues, that poor thing." She looked up at Luke who was standing there, his face white and his jaw clenched.

"You'd never guess," he said, his voice gruff.

"I know. Chase did a wonderful job raising her. I think we were able to help give her some security, knowing that there were people who were still her family and who she could count on. My parents consider her their granddaughter."

He looked down at the table. "Your parents are good people."

Her heart squeezed at the emotion in his voice. He looked back up at her. "You're a good woman, Gwen."

He held her gaze and she wanted to know what that look was in his eyes. She had no idea what he was thinking, what he was feeling, but the air in the room had changed. It wasn't filled with humor anymore and it wasn't sexual tension, but it was distinct. Almost heavy.

"Auntie Gwen! I'm ready for bed!" Maggie yelling at the top of her lungs shattered the moment, drowning out whatever was happening.

"I'll go tuck her in. Why don't you pour us some wine? Julia left a bottle on the kitchen island."

"Will do," he said, putting the lid on the Monopoly box.

She sprinted up the stairs and into Maggie's room. Sure enough, Maggie was tucked under her plush pink duvet and cover. "Did you have fun tonight?"

Maggie nodded emphatically. "I like him. A lot. I'd say he's a keeper."

Gwen laughed, sitting on the edge of her bed. "I agree."

Once she finished reading Maggie her story, she kissed

her on the forehead, turned out her beside lamp, and said goodnight.

"Auntie Gwen?" Maggie called out as she was almost out the door.

"Yes, sweetie?" she asked, holding on to the doorframe.

"I'm happy you have a boyfriend. Now all the grown-ups in our family will be happy."

Gwen smiled at the little girl, feeling it too. Maybe they would all finally be happy.

She walked back into the living room and Luke was standing there, pouring wine. He'd lit the fireplace and turned off the large dining room chandelier over the table. Her heart started a frantic rhythm as he crossed the room and handed her a glass. He was looking less rumpled than she was used to. Tonight he was wearing dark jeans and a navy V-necked sweater with a white T-shirt underneath. He still had his trademark stubble and his hair was still slightly rumpled, just the way she preferred it, she discovered.

"She's asleep?"

Gwen nodded. "Either that or she's eavesdropping at the top of the stairs."

They both laughed and sat on the couch together. Tonight, she was determined to know more about him. "How's your sister?"

He took a sip of wine, but not before she caught the tightening of his jaw. "She's okay. She's dealing with some stuff she's not letting me in on, but I don't want to pressure her. She'll let me know when she's ready."

Not much insight. "So…it's just the two of you?"

He gave a nod. "Our dad left when we were little and our mother raised us. She, uh, died five years ago. Cancer."

She reached out and grabbed his hand, hating how vulnerable he sounded when he spoke about his mother. "I'm sorry to hear that."

"Thanks," he said, clearing his throat.

"Were you close?"

He nodded. "Yeah. The three of us were very close. Things didn't go as planned five years ago and I regret not having more time—more good time with her at the end."

Her throat ached as she watched him trying to hide his emotion. "It's so hard to know how long we have together and to remember to enjoy the little things, isn't it? The week Michael and Matthew died I was so consumed by my college courses that I remember I kept putting off seeing them. I kept saying how busy I was, and I believed it. And then that was it, they were gone," she whispered, quickly taking a sip of her wine. She and Michael had always gotten along. He'd been a good big brother—he'd led them all well, looked out for all of them.

"I'm sorry," he said gruffly, reaching out and placing his strong hand on the nape of her neck. There was so much pain in his eyes and she hated that they both had regrets, that they had both lost people very precious to them.

"She died five years ago. Did she know about Lisa?"

He pulled his hand away and rubbed the back of his neck. She hated asking him these questions but she was desperate to know the details, to really know him. "Yeah. I think that was too much for her to handle." He looked like he wanted to say something else, she sensed that there was so much more than he was letting her in on. But he didn't speak. Instead, a flash of vulnerability flickered across his eyes.

"I'm so sorry she had to go through that on top of dealing with her cancer. We can't go back, Luke. She must have had so much faith in you, in the kind of man you'd become. She must have been so proud of you. A lot of people use what happens in their childhood as an excuse to not amount to anything. Look at you, you're an incredible doctor, a wonderful brother."

He ducked his head, but didn't seem comforted by

anything she was saying. "You have this amazing ability to see the good in people and situations, Gwen."

"Not always, but I know a great guy when I see one." His head turned sharply to her, the lines around his mouth pronounced and it looked as though, for a moment, he was going to say something, disagree or something. When he said nothing after a moment, she asked him another question. "Do you ever see your father?"

He shook his head. "When he left, he left for good. I was ten. Haley was four. It forced me to grow up. I remember my mother sitting at the kitchen table that first night, just crying. She had no idea how she was going to pay for rent, for groceries."

She placed her hand on his leg and squeezed.

"But she did. We cut out everything that wasn't a must. She got a second job and I stayed home with Haley, at night, even though she didn't want to leave us without a sitter. I insisted. I told her we were a team and I could be the other parent. As soon as Haley could be left home alone, I got a part-time job...I haven't thought about this in years."

"But she sounds like she was an amazing woman."

"My mother was an incredibly strong woman and she didn't deserve to go out the way she did. She deserved to see her children happily married. She deserved to see grandchildren."

She put down her wine glass and wrapped her arms around him. "She's watching you, Luke. She knows how amazing her son is."

She felt him put down his wine glass and then wrap his arms around her, burying his face in her neck. "I have no idea how you do that, Gwen. I have no idea how you actually make me believe in something I don't."

She felt such empathy for him, for what he'd been through. He pulled away, his hand still on her nape, still holding her close, his gaze filled with something she didn't understand completely. Before she had time to dwell on it, he lowered his mouth to hers, brushing his lips over hers gently and then capturing her mouth in a sweet kiss that turned into so much more. He leaned back into the couch, taking her with him. When they heard the slamming of a car door outside, they both reluctantly pulled apart. "I guess they're back," she said, smoothing her hair and sweater.

"Maybe that's a good thing," he said.

"Are you all ready for your sister?"

He shrugged. "Well, I have a house."

Alarm bells were starting to go off. "I mean like her room and stuff. If she's leaving her husband, and driving here, she's probably not bringing a lot of stuff with her."

He was starting to look confused. "So?"

She tried to be patient. "Maybe we should go shopping tomorrow. Let's get some accessories for her room, to make her welcome and cheer her up."

He still looked clueless. "Sure…accessories."

She let out a sigh of exasperation. "Flowers, maybe a new duvet cover, pillows, some magazines, maybe a small desk and chair, a lamp…"

Her voice trailed off at his expression. She couldn't quite figure it out.

He coughed. "Okay."

"You *did* graduate med school, right?"

He threw back his head and laughed, snatching her wrist and kissing her. She laughed along with him, glad he could take teasing. "I think you and my sister will really like each other."

"I'm sure we will. Okay, so I'll make a list of places to go and items to buy. Tell me everything you know about her. Does she like antiques? I know this great little indoor flea market and they have tons of cute shabby chic things."

He didn't look impressed. "Shabby what?"

She rolled her eyes and patted his hand. "Don't worry, it'll be okay."

Chase and Julia walked in a few minutes later. "Hey, how was your night out?"

"Great," Julia said, hanging up her coat. "How did you two manage?"

"Maggie is a really great kid," Luke, said, surprising her.

"Thanks," Chase said, pride stamped across this handsome face.

After they said their good-byes, Luke walked her out to her car. "What time do you want me to pick you up tomorrow?"

She sat down, trying not to look like she was disappointed that he was ending the evening. "How about noon?"

"Perfect," he said, leaning down for a quick kiss.

She gave him a wave and shut the door, desperate to be by herself.

After he pulled out of the driveway she did a quick replay of the last five minutes of their conversation, wondering if something had gone wrong. Maybe he was having second thoughts? Maybe he thought things were moving too quickly. Or maybe he felt uncomfortable because he'd revealed so much about himself tonight. That had to be it. It couldn't have anything to do with his feelings for her…or lack of.

Chapter Eight

"So this is shabby shit?"

Gwen slapped her hands over her mouth and turned to him, her eyes wide and filled with laughter. He ignored the saleswoman in the booth who was frowning fiercely at him. What the hell?

"Chic. Shabby *chic.*"

He grinned. "Oh." He thought it best not to mention that none of this crap looked particularly chic. It was used and the paint was chipping off. They were standing in what had to be the tenth booth featuring furniture that looked exactly like the previous nine booths. Really, he wanted to spend the day with Gwen. Even though he should be spending less time with her, he was spending more.

He kept telling himself he'd tell her the truth, but the churning in his gut always stopped him, reminding him that the second he did that, she would walk out on his life. So what options did he have really? Just enjoy his time with her.

"I'm thinking this cute powder-blue desk with that white chair we saw at the last booth. They will look great with the white nightstand we saw at the first booth. Then we get the powder-blue and white paisley quilt we saw at the third booth." She smiled up at him.

She must have been waiting for a reply. "I have no idea what you just said."

She rolled her eyes at him and tugged him along where they spent the next half hour buying all the stuff she mentioned and then loading it into his SUV. "You do have a bed for her, right?" she asked once he closed the trunk.

"A bed?"

She put her head in her hands. "Seriously? Get in the car, we need to get a bed and mattress. And pillows."

He grinned. He liked the bossy side of Gwen. "You're very hot when you're barking out orders," he said, tugging her into him.

She frowned. "I don't bark."

"Kind of," he said, smiling as he leaned down to kiss her. "Well, you'll be pleased to know I'm not completely incompetent. There is a double bed in the spare room."

"I'm impressed," she said, patting his shoulder like he was a first grader.

They spent the rest of the day running errands, Gwen coming up with stuff he hadn't even thought of. When they were finally back at his place, she took charge and started setting up his sister's room. "You don't have to do all this you know. It's your day off."

She straightened up from smoothing out the quilt on the bed and he forced his eyes from her very cute ass and up to her eyes. He needed to keep things from moving too fast. Or whatever it was he was doing. "I'm happy to help. I like decorating. So what do you think?" she asked, lifted her arms and spreading them wide. He thought she was hot. And gorgeous. And kind. And he thought that he was the biggest ass for knowing all of that and wanting her anyway.

He didn't want to be standing here talking about decorating when there was a bed in the room. He wanted to be in the bed, with Gwen. What kind of sick demented situation had he gotten himself into? The one woman he wanted more than anyone was the one woman he couldn't have, but he couldn't get enough of her, so he kept agreeing to these PG visits.

"Hello?" she asked when he hadn't answered yet. "Don't you think this room is gorgeous? I hope she likes it. I mean what if she has your taste? She'll hate it."

He managed a smile. "She doesn't have my taste. This looks exactly like something Haley would like."

"Good. I can't wait to meet her. I should probably get going, I have a bunch of errands to run. Baby shower stuff. Then I need to get some food to my friend. Oh, hey, before I forget, do you want to go skating Friday night?" She crossed the small room to stand in front of him.

"Uh, no."

She frowned at him, clearly not insecure in his feelings for her. He liked that. "Well, we're going skating Friday night because we're actually really lucky the outdoor rink is still open this close to spring."

He tried to hide his smile. "Lucky according to who?"

She poked him in the stomach. "Seriously, you'll love it. Can you take Friday night off?"

He'd take off any night for her. Just not skating. "I haven't been on skates since high school."

She smiled, like maybe she liked that, or that she was anticipating watching him fall flat on his ass. "Don't worry, I'll help you. Consider it payback for you helping me when I was sick."

"I think the term you're looking for is returning the favor…I believe payback implies something sinister."

She patted his shoulder. "It'll be okay."

He was laughing when he bent down to kiss her. "Fine. Skating on Friday."

The knocking on the door prevented him from figuring out how he was going to stop kissing her. Before he could even walk out of the room, the door opened, followed by the sound of his sister. "Hello, Luke!"

Suddenly his sister threw herself at him. He held her close, deciding he'd reprimand her for not giving him any warning later.

"I made it!"

He heard the relief in her voice, combined with happiness. He hated that she had been through something traumatic. He wouldn't press right away but over the next few days he'd find out what had happened with her husband. She finally pulled away and he got a good look at her. They were similar in coloring, but she had dark circles under her eyes and her face was pale. She looked as though she'd lost a significant amount of weight too. He clenched his teeth, trying to control the anger he felt toward her loser ex. "Glad you made it in record time."

"Hi," his sister said, spotting Gwen. "You must be Gwen."

"Hi, you must be Haley," Gwen said. Instead of reaching out to shake his sister's hand, she pulled her into a hug. "I'm so glad you came to stay with your brother."

Holy hell. His gut tightened and his throat constricted as he saw tears form in his sister's eyes. Gwen was so damn sweet. "And I'm so happy you're in my brother's life, I've heard so much about you," she said, shooting him her trademark badass little sister grin.

Gwen looked surprised. "I'm surprised he mentioned me.
"

"Oh, he talks about you all the time," Haley said.

"You too. We just finished decorating your room because he had no idea what to do." They both burst out laughing.

"Standing right here," he said, happy as hell and awed that Gwen had already made his sister laugh.

"I can't wait to see it!" Haley said, and the two of them started walking down the hall.

"Do you like your room?" Gwen asked, completely ignoring him as Haley stood in the doorway of the guest bedroom.

Haley looked around, judging by the huge smile on her face totally loved it. "It's so nice. Honestly, I was expecting a sleeping bag on the ground," she said with a snort.

Gwen nodded sympathetically. "Yeah, I kind of nudged him in the right direction. I had a feeling he was going to drop the ball."

"Sometimes I worry about him. Like does he remember to eat?"

"It's amazing they let me in the ER to oh, I don't know, *save lives*, when I'm such an idiot," he said. Their opinion of him was a little shocking. Instead of either of them looking the least bit sheepish, they burst out laughing.

"Well, it was great meeting you, Haley. I'm going to head out," Gwen said, and they started walking toward the door. He followed. He had known they'd get along but seeing them together made him realize how great Gwen would be for Haley. She was loyal and caring and that was what his sister needed. He needed Gwen. He wished he'd met her when he was younger, before anything had happened, maybe then things would have been different.

"You don't have to leave because I'm here," Haley said.

"No, you guys need to catch up. Besides, I have a million things to do and this is my only day off. Oh, also, in case Luke forgets to tell you, you're invited to my parents place for Sunday night dinner," Gwen said, pulling on her coat.

His gut clenched. Right. Sunday night with all of them.

His sister was smiling again. "Thank you so much. I'd love

to."

"I'll walk you out," he said.

Haley rolled her suitcase to the bedroom. "Bye, Gwen!"

Once the two of them were outside, he grabbed her hand, needing to make contact with her.

"Your sister seems really great."

He blew out a breath. "She is. Thank you for being so nice to her."

"She's hurting though, you can see it," she said, concern in her eyes as she stopped at her car.

He agreed. He'd seen the same thing. She had put on a brave front, but he could tell. "I know." He'd deal with Haley when he went back inside. Now he wanted a few moments of just Gwen.

"So, anyway, I'd better get going," she said, looking unsure of herself.

It was his fault. He was being a prick because he didn't know what to do. He wanted Gwen in every possible way, but he was torn between hurting her now and hurting her later. He put his hand on her car door and raised one hand to the nape of her neck. Her breath caught. "Gwen, I'm sorry our day was cut short."

She shrugged. "Not a problem. We are just friends anyway."

"We're so beyond friends," he said, lowering his head. "You're the best thing I've ever known," he whispered before kissing her. Kissing Gwen seemed inevitable, since every time he saw her, he wanted to kiss her. Not kissing her was becoming impossible. She kissed him back with the same need he felt and soon what was meant to be a quick kiss turned into something much more. They both had layers of clothes on and it was snowing and his sister was inside the house. She pulled away first.

"I'd better get going."

"Gwen," he said roughly, not knowing what to say to her, yet not wanting to leave things like this.

"Yes?" she asked, hope lighting her eyes. Hope in him was always a mistake.

"I'll see you in a bit," he said, leaning down for one quick kiss before shutting her door. He stepped back and watched her pull away, giving one final wave as she drove off. The distinct feeling in his gut that he was about to destroy everything made him feel sick.

He glanced back at the cabin, took a deep breath, and went to join his sister inside. When he walked in, he spotted her standing by the large window in the family room.

"Not bad, Luke. It's gorgeous out here. I think I could get used to this cold because of the view."

He'd grown accustomed to Montana and the winters. "Yeah, it's pretty cool, especially after a snowstorm."

"Wow, look at you appreciating nature," she said, walking toward him.

His gut churned because now that her coat was off he noticed she looked like a skeleton. He knew she was forcing herself to appear happy. She wasn't fooling him. "I'm just repeating crap I overhear."

She laughed and hit him on the shoulder. "I absolutely love Gwen. She's perfect for you!"

He winced. "Don't want to talk about it. But yeah, Gwen's great. Are you hungry?" he asked, hoping to change the subject. "If you would have told me you were coming, I would have gotten some food."

"You can't cook. Also, we will come back to the topic of Gwen."

He ignored the Gwen comment. "I'm too busy to cook, but I would have bought food. You want a pizza? There's a great pizza place in town and maybe if I offer the guy extra, he'll deliver out here."

Her stomach growled and she nodded. "Done. Extra cheese. Extra pepperoni."

That was more like it. He placed the order and after agreeing to pay Luigi's kid an extra ten bucks to drive out there, they sat in the family room. Even though it was small, the ceilings were vaulted and all the wood beams exposed. If he was into this kind of thing, he'd say it was a pretty perfect room. His sister snuggled up under a blanket and settled onto the couch opposite him. "Well, look at us, together again, our lives in shambles. Who would have thought, huh?"

The sadness in her voice prompted him to make light of it. "So you were young and picked a douche of a husband. It's not a big deal." But it was. They had both picked the wrong partners. If he'd been married to Gwen, his life would never have gone down that road. He couldn't have seen himself as the man he used to be. But that wasn't Lisa's fault; it was his own. If he had met Gwen back then, they never would have worked. It had made him question his own ability to read people.

It was also a reminder of his own failings. He'd failed his wife. He'd been an equal if not greater screw-up in their marriage. It made him question the entire damn institution, which presented another problem. It's not that he'd even consider getting married again, but there was something about Gwen that made a guy think about marriage. She was the real deal. She was the kind of woman he should have looked for in the beginning, but maybe he wasn't ready for a woman like her then. His priorities had been very different. Gwen had made it very clear she wanted the whole package, marriage and kids. He could never be a father again.

Haley's eyes filled with tears. "You warned me, though. How come I didn't see it?"

He paused for a second, hating that he had to ask, bracing himself for her answer. "What did he do, Haley?"

She turned from him and shook her head. "I can't talk about it yet."

He leaned forward, trying to still look calm. "Do you need me to hurt him?"

She laughed and he smiled with her. "Do you want a hot drink or something?"

"You learned how to make coffee?"

He frowned. "You know I am an adult, right? And a doctor?"

Her brow stayed lifted.

He leaned back in his chair. "Fine. It's a Keurig, but it still counts as making coffee."

She laughed again.

"So, coffee? Tea?"

"Coffee," she said. "Always coffee."

He stood and prepped two cups for them. "Oh, I don't have any milk or cream."

"Omigod, Luke. How can I have coffee without dairy?"

His sister had always been picky. "Like I said, if you'd told me you were coming today, I would have bought some."

"Fine, fine. I'll take it black."

He walked back to the couches and handed her a cup.

"So tell me what you've been up to. Please tell me the reason you and Gwen are hanging out and kissing like teenagers at her car is because you've told her the truth and as I've predicted, she accepts that it was an accident and all is well with the world."

He leaned forward, bracing his forearms on his legs. "No."

She groaned. "Why?"

"I…I've become involved with Gwen without telling any of them the truth," he said, his voice sounding strange to his ears. He regretted telling her the minute the words came out of his mouth. Her theatrical gasp solidified how stupid he was to tell her anything.

She raised her hand to her heart. "Oh, Luke. What a tangled web we weave."

"Seriously."

She shrugged. "Sorry, it seemed like the perfect time to use that expression."

"It wasn't supposed to happen like this. I wasn't supposed to get to know her, but I did and now…"

"Please don't tell me you've slept together."

"I'm not a total douche."

"You're not a douche at all," she said, with a look that told him she clearly pitied him. "You know what I think of all this already. You know you're not responsible, right? Wrong place, wrong time, it could have been anyone, Luke."

He stared down at the ground. Yeah he'd played this game with her before, but it didn't matter because it *had* been him, no one else. If he had done things differently then maybe Gwen's brother and nephew would still be alive. Lisa and their baby would have been alive. "Well, we've been over this before. I am to blame for the condition I was in when I got behind the wheel that night."

"Stop saying that as though you were a drunk driver! You were a tired doctor, you were a husband fighting with his wife, and the road conditions were bad."

"I could have slept at the hospital."

"Stop it. Stop it. You've blamed yourself for five years. I understand needing to come out here and meet these people and apologize, I do. But what you've done now by getting to know them and getting involved with this Gwen woman is setting yourself up for disaster. How the heck is she going to feel when you tell her the truth?"

He didn't say anything, just gripped his coffee mug tight. He had no idea. He had no answers to any of her irritating, if not completely relevant, questions. "I don't know."

"Luke, you have to tell her."

The doorbell rang and his sister jumped up. Pizza time. It took him a moment to get up, to shed the weight of the new burden that was now on his shoulders. He wanted time with Gwen. He wanted to know her, everything about her in every possible way, even if it meant that she'd hate him in the end. He just wanted time before he saw hatred in her eyes, before everything was ruined.

Chapter Nine

"You're afraid, aren't you?" Gwen said as they each laced up their rented skates. He laughed, despite the insult.

They were sitting on one of the green park benches surrounding the open-air skating rink. It was one of those perfect, Norman Rockwell scenes. There were vendors selling hot chocolate and warm pretzels and popcorn. Kids were skating. Families were laughing. Snow was falling gently. But it was the woman beside him who made it all mean something.

He glanced over at her and she was giving him an adorable smirk, so he leaned forward, laughing despite himself, and kissed it away. When he pulled back and looked into her eyes, he kind of knew she had him. Somehow, Gwen had managed to cut through everything he'd been hiding behind. Gwen made him believe that maybe he could have a second chance…at everything.

"Let's go, Muffin Man," she said, jumping up. Her hands were on her hips and she had no issues balancing on her skates. Her dark hair was long and loose under her white beanie. Her nose was pink already and her cheeks were rosy. She was the most beautiful woman he'd ever seen. But he knew that alone wasn't what got him, it was her whole package. It was the person he knew she was inside.

He stood slowly, aware of his lack of expertise in this area. "You know, judging by that grin on your face, you're looking forward to seeing me fall on my ass."

Her eyes sparkled as she held out her hand for him. "Only kind of."

He laughed again and took her hand, needing it for support as they made their way to the rink. He stepped on the ice tentatively. Two teenagers zipped by him and he fell backward with a thud and maybe an expletive that was a tad too loud.

Gwen held out her hand and to her credit did a fine job trying not to laugh.

"Look, it's Dr. Thomson! He fell on his bum!"

He swore under his breath and managed to stand and not fall as he heard the boy. Gwen was wiping tears from her eyes while taking heaving breaths in between laughs as a little boy and his parents skated over to them. Gwen held his arm, sort of bracing him up. Great. Pity was written all over her pretty features.

"Hello, Dr. Thomson! Remember us? You treated Chris for pneumonia last month."

He smiled at the family. He did remember them. They'd come in during the night when their six-year-old son had been wheezing and crying. "Yes, I do. You're all looking well. Chris, all better?"

The little boy nodded. "Thanks to you!"

"Well, we won't keep you. Have a good night," the father said, and they skated away. He stood there for a second, and he realized that for the first time, he liked being part of a community. That was new for him. He hated being attached. He hated running into patients. But this…was nice. He looked over at Gwen. She wasn't pitying him anymore. She was looking at him with something that made him wish for things like he was a kid again.

"I think one of the most attractive things about you, despite the obvious, um, external attributes you have," she said, turning into him, holding onto the front of his jacket. "Is that you have this warmth and compassion. It's there, under all those layers of hurt, but it's there."

He leaned down and kissed her, not caring that they were in a public place. He kissed her because he couldn't not kiss her. He couldn't not fall for Gwen. No matter how hard he tried not to, he was falling in love with her.

• • •

Gwen pulled back from Luke and smiled up at him. She couldn't stop smiling tonight. Something felt different, like he was opening up and all of this was real. "C'mon, time to skate," she said. She skated a circle around him, while he just stood there looking hot, irritated, and amused.

"You're a show-off, Gwen." He was grinning when he said it.

"True enough. Consider this payback for all those weeks of ignoring me. Here, let me help you skate."

"What are you doing?" he asked, when she placed her hands on his back.

"I'm helping you move. I'm going to push you slowly. Try not to fall. Bend at the knees a little. You look a little stiff."

"I'm not a giant statue you can push along the ice."

She moved beside him. "Okay, give me your hand and I'll pull you."

He sighed and accepted her hand, but she could tell he was fighting a smile. They slowly made their way around the ice, staying to the edges so people could pass them. She couldn't have asked for a better night. They talked and laughed as they circled the ice. Everything about tonight reaffirmed what she knew the first day she met him—she and TMM were meant to be.

"We need hot chocolate," he said as they approached the hot chocolate booth. "And any other stuff he's selling."

"Fine. I'll get it. You stand still. Don't move."

"Agreed."

"Oh, you know what? I left my purse in the car."

"Obviously, I'll pay. I can't move, but I'll pay. Here, take my wallet." He moved to grab it but he looked like he was going to fall over with the motion.

"I'll get it," she said, reaching around him. "Though I think this is a ploy to get me to grab your butt."

"Kind of is," he said, giving her a kiss as she slipped the wallet out of the back pocket of his jeans. She was not going to let her fingers linger on what she already knew was a pretty fine butt.

"Don't move," she said, skating in the direction of the chocolate booth. She ordered them two hot chocolates and one chocolate donut. She opened his wallet and searched for the correct bill. She paused as her finger felt something in the back of the bills. She paused at what looked like an ultrasound picture. Her heart slammed up into her throat. This was his private wallet. She glanced down at the picture for a moment, confirming it was indeed an ultrasound of a baby. Whose was it? He said he didn't have kids. She knew his sister didn't have kids. She glanced over at him, waving as he smiled and waved back at her.

She paid for their drinks and food and made her way back to the rink. This wasn't her business. It had nothing to do with her. When he was ready, he'd open up about whatever else he had in his past. All she knew to be true right now, was that Luke made her feel like no guy ever had. He was funny, kind, loving, and sexy as hell. He made her feel alive and special. She was prepared to fall in love, all the way, with him, no matter the cost.

Gwen gave herself a quick check in the rearview mirror, and satisfied there were no major flaws with her face or hair, decided it was time to go and surprise Luke. She didn't know if this was a good idea or not, and she imagined it was pretty hectic in the ER and he probably wouldn't welcome any intrusion, but when she heard he was pulling a double shift, she felt bad. He probably had to do this because he'd spent so many nights with her when she had the flu and then when she'd made him take the night off for skating. Her discovery of the ultrasound picture in his wallet the other night only made her want to get to know him more. She trusted him. She trusted that when he was ready, he'd fill in all the missing pieces of his life story for her.

She grabbed the paper bag that contained a few sweets from her shop and then the other paper bag that had two slices of Luigi's pizza. She walked across the parking lot as quickly as she could without jeopardizing all the goodies she was holding. The emergency room doors slid open as she crossed the threshold and she walked toward the information desk.

"Hi there," she said to the pretty woman behind the desk. "I'm just dropping off some food for a…friend…who works here. Dr. Thomson."

The woman sat up a little straighter and seemed to give Gwen a once-over from her barely-able-to-see-over-the-counter posture. "Oh, you're friends with Dr. Thomson?"

Gwen tried not to let her irritation show. She didn't want to add to any kind of hospital gossip. But seriously, all the women in this hospital were interested in him? Last time the nurse. This time, this lady. "Yes. I have dinner for him."

"Oh, well you can leave it with me and I can put it in the doctor's lunchroom and let him know it's there."

Was this woman screening his visitors? "Well…do you know if he's going on break soon?"

She snorted. "He never goes on break. It's cold and flu season, do you know how backed up that place is?"

Gwen frowned and looked in the direction of the ER waiting room. She grimaced and tried not to inhale too deeply. "Okay," she said, reluctantly sliding the coffee and paper bags across the counter.

"And who shall I say sent this?"

"Um, Gwen."

"Do you have a last name?" she asked, pointing her pen to a notepad.

"Bailey."

"All right, Gwen Bailey. I will make sure he gets it."

"Thanks," she said, slowly leaving the hospital entrance. That wasn't exactly the way she'd planned for that to go. The disappointment didn't go away when she got to her car, either. As she made her way back to her car, she wondered about their night, or rather nights, together when she was sick. Now, it was as though he'd disappeared. Was he having second thoughts? Maybe…

"Gwen!"

She spun around, her heart beating a mile a minute as she spotting him jogging across the parking lot. Omg, the hotness of him. She hadn't ever seen him dressed in scrubs before. His tall, athletic frame seemed to make those scrubs into the sexiest getup she'd ever seen. His arms were bare and she could make out the well-defined biceps. But when her eyes managed to meet his, she felt a twinge of sympathy for him. He looked wiped.

"How did you know I was here?" she asked.

He didn't answer. Instead, he closed the remaining distance between them. He wrapped her up, backed her up until she was sandwiched between her car and him, and all she could think about was how good he tasted and felt. He kissed her as though he was starved and she was dinner. He held her as though she was his lifeline. They kissed until a car horn honked and a man poked his head out the window. "Are you going to move your car? I need a parking spot."

"Go to the back lot and walk," Luke said. She let out a startled laugh as the man gave Luke the finger and drove away.

"I didn't want to bother you, but I felt bad, and I know how crappy hospital cafeteria food is," she said.

He grinned. "I'm not complaining. You're the best thing I've seen in twelve hours."

"Can you go home?"

"Yeah. I'm ready to go. I just need to grab my things, and dinner, and I'm outta here."

"Do you want to come back to my place?" she asked, not believing she'd asked that. The look in his eyes told her that's exactly where he wanted to go.

"I'll meet you there. I'm just going to grab a quick shower," he said. He gave her a long kiss and then was gone, jogging back across the lot and then vanishing into the hospital.

Gwen took a deep breath as she got into her car. Then, once the door was shut, squealed with happiness. It was her year. It was true. She was finally taking all the steps to claim her happiness. Then panic set in. She drove out of that hospital like a speed demon. She had so much to do. Body parts needed shaving. Her apartment needed cleaning. Candles. She needed to light candles. Wine. Did she have any wine? Her mind was racing a mile a minute as she pulled into her spot outside the building.

Once inside the apartment, she decided showering and shaving were priority one. Once she did that as quickly as possible, she ran around the apartment cleaning up. Her hair was still wet when she ran into her bedroom to try and decide on what to wear. Okay, new underwear and bra, check. Then it was the rest…she didn't want to look as though she was trying too hard, but she also wanted to look as though she was putting some effort into it.

Panic was rising in as she tore through her clothes, but then couldn't make a mess because he'd be here any minute. Finally, she decided on jeans, because hello they weren't yoga pants, but still weren't too overdone. Then she picked out a white looks-like-cashmere sweater, but then decided against it because what if she spilled red wine? That was a very real possibility for her. Red. She should wear red. Perfect. She slipped on the red looks-like-cashmere sweater that she'd bought on her shopping spree. It had a V-neck that wasn't low, but showed a hint of skin. She spun around and gave herself a look in the mirror. Okay. She tousled her hair a little, hating that she didn't have time to properly dry it. Candles and wine.

She ran out into the kitchen and took out her matches and lit the three candles on the coffee table in the family room. She stood and her heart started pounding as she spotted Luke's SUV parked across the street. She walked over to the window when she noticed he was still inside. It looked like he was looking at his phone or something. He wasn't moving though. He slowly lowered his head and placed it on the steering wheel. Worry shot through her.

Was he having second thoughts?

Or maybe the poor guy was just so wiped and needed a nap. Had she forced this whole thing on him? Had she come on too strong?

Oh, the humiliation of it all…

· · ·

"We don't want you to contact us again, Luke. We made it clear how we feel. These letters and phone calls of apology mean nothing to us. You were responsible for our daughter, for that baby, and you failed. We will never understand how you were only able to save yourself and not them. My wife can't get out of bed most days because of depression since we lost Lisa. Your contact only makes it worse. Leave us alone."

Luke heard the click on the other end of the line and squeezed his eyes shut, trying to breathe, but it was more like wheezing. He tossed his phone onto the dashboard and slowly put his head on the steering wheel and squeezed his eyes shut as tears spilled from the corners.

You should have known, Luke. Every time he'd tried to contact his former in-laws during the last five years, he had gotten the same kind of thing. The night he'd had to call them from the accident site had almost killed him. He'd stood, ambulances and police surrounding the scene of the accident. The rain had turned to sleet and he'd called, sputtering out the words that no parent should ever have to hear. Luke didn't know what he'd expected of them, but they blamed him. They had never stopped blaming him. It had been a year since he'd contacted them, so he wasn't quite sure what had prompted him to call them now. Well, if he was honest with himself, he did know—it was Gwen. He wanted closure, he wanted to start over, wanted their forgiveness, finally. He wanted a sign that maybe he could tell Gwen the truth and she'd forgive him too.

You're acting like a naïve idiot.

He lifted his head and ran his hands down his face, knowing he should go up there and cancel on Gwen. He was in no condition to be with her tonight; he needed to be by himself with a bottle of anything. He got out of his car and crossed the road, the weight of the last five years crushing him. He had made so many attempts at change, had tried to be a better man, had tried to help as many people as possible, but none of it was good enough. None of it would ever erase that at a critical point in his life, he wasn't good enough.

He climbed the stairs to Gwen's apartment, fully intending on telling her that he was too wiped from work and that he just needed to go home and sleep, but she was standing at the top of the stairs. He stopped, shaken to the core by what she was unknowingly offering him, maybe what she had always been offering him.

Gwen was his solace; she was his redeemer.

He wanted in on everything her warm eyes promised. He wanted in on everything she offered him. He wanted one night to be the man that she thought he was, the man he wanted to be. He wanted one night to show her what she meant to him, just how deeply she affected him.

"You okay?" she whispered.

He didn't answer right away, memorizing the way she looked at him, the way she was dressed, the tilt of her full lips as she smiled. He wasn't okay, hadn't been okay for the last five years, but being with Gwen was the closest he'd ever get to being whole again.

He paused, before reaching that top step so that she was at eye level. He didn't want to think anymore, he didn't want to acknowledge how he didn't deserve Gwen in his life, or what would happen later. Right now, more than anything, he needed to feel again.

"I need you," he said, the confession a surprise to him and her. He raised his hands, slowly tangling them in her hair as he lowered his head and kissed her. "I need you more than I've ever needed anyone," he whispered against her mouth. She made a small sound and then wrapped her arms around his neck and he lifted her, walking into her apartment and shutting the door with his foot. Gwen kissed him back like she needed him just as much.

• • •

Luke followed her down and covered her with his hard body. She hadn't known exactly what would happen tonight, but never in a million years did she expect him to walk up those stairs and look at her like she was his lifeblood. And that kiss…the current kisses he was placing down her neck were more than she knew what to do with. In all her twenty-something years, she had never experienced anything as powerful as Luke.

Her clothes fell away but he kept coming back to her mouth, kissing her slow and deep, as though he needed to savor. She tugged his shirt off and ran her hands down the sinewy length of his arms, then up his shoulders and down his chest. His skin was hot to the touch and flexed as her fingers explored him. Luke was breathtaking. Before he lowered his head to kiss her again, she caught the look in his eyes, understood the hunger, and understood the longing. Finally, she understood what it meant to want to be with someone so completely. Her body reacted to him, to every touch and kiss, as though it were desperate for him. And it was, she was. She was so desperate for everything Luke was offering, and everything he wasn't.

She welcomed him with everything she had, with all her doubts and insecurities, and with all the love she already had for this man. She welcomed him, surrendering the fear that this would be fleeting, that this feeling, this fire, this connection was too good to be true.

• • •

Luke stared at the dark ceiling in Gwen's bedroom. Her

naked body was wrapped around him, and the perfection of an hour ago was fading fast, replaced by an alarming amount of self-loathing. He had come here tonight, selfishly needing Gwen, selfishly taking what he needed. He'd known, from very early on how good they would be together. But he hadn't counted on how good. Or that there would be an emotional connection that scared the crap out of him because when she found out the truth, he'd have to find a way to live without her.

"Why do you look like you are having regrets?"

He started, looking down at Gwen. He had no idea she'd woken up. The vulnerability in her eyes made guilt stir inside him. Regrets. Yeah. Where did he start? He didn't want to break her heart. He didn't want to be the ass who walked out of here, but he was going to break her heart eventually. "No regrets," he said, then pressed a kiss to her head. The last thing he wanted her to think was that he had doubts about her. "Maybe I wish that you'd have let me in on the fact that you've never slept with anyone before."

She inhaled sharply and her eyes filled with tears. Crap. He didn't want her to cry. "You weren't supposed to notice."

He cleared his throat, knowing he was going to have to tread carefully. "I would have probably done things a little differently."

She blinked and her tears were gone, replaced by a smile that effectively filled his male ego, along with assuaging that part of his guilt. "I wouldn't have wanted anything to go differently. You were the one. I mean, not *the* one. After you leave Shadow Creek, I will have to find more ones, but you were the first one. But don't worry, no pressure or anything. Really, it was a matter of opportunity or lack of. I mean I was living with my parents. And I had no life for the last five years. Before that wasn't convenient either."

Well, hell. He didn't even know where to start with that

one. He had come to recognize that Gwen made him feel all the things. She made him analyze his life, his emotions. She made him question all his stupid beliefs. She made it clear to him that she knew a hell of a lot more about how to live life than he did. She had this energy, this light that he wanted to share. She made him want the white picket fence, no matter how undeserving he was.

And he wanted to be the guy, the only guy in her life, but he had no right. "Thanks. I think. Also, I'm glad I showed up at a convenient time in your schedule."

She placed her hand on his chest and perched her chin on top, her brown eyes sparkled and she gave him a smile that made him want to forget all the reasons he should leave. Who was he fooling? He wasn't leaving her tonight. She must have had the same thoughts, because as he threaded his fingers through her hair, she had already met him halfway. He kissed her, memorizing every sound, every taste, every inch of her, knowing this woman had changed him forever.

Chapter Ten

"So, are you going to tell Gwen tonight?"

Luke gripped the steering wheel tightly as he drove toward the Bailey's home the next Sunday night. "Yeah, I'm planning on telling everyone at Sunday night dinner."

"No need for sarcasm, just wondering what your plans are. Continue to get close to this family and Gwen and then tell them? Maybe when Gwen tells you she's in love with you and wants you to father her children. Tell her then."

"When did you get so sarcastic?"

"*Are* you going to tell her?"

"Yes, I'm just waiting for the right time."

"Omigod," she groaned, throwing up her hands, nearly hitting him in the confined space of the SUV. "What are you waiting for? This is only going to get worse. You need to tell her."

"I know."

"You still haven't slept with her, right?"

"Can you stop asking me that?" He had slept with her, without telling her everything, and that was unforgivable. It put him in the biggest douche category and he didn't know if she'd ever forgive him for that. Even after tonight he had no idea what she'd do.

She made her trademark snorting sound. "I'm looking out for her. I think Gwen is great for you. I haven't seen you laugh in years. You even walk around the house smiling. She makes you happy. I don't want you to screw this up so badly that you lose her, because that would be a really douchey thing to do."

"Thanks." His sister and Gwen got along great. Gwen had come by the other night and they'd ordered pizza and the two of them had forced him to watch a sappy movie. He also found out that his sister had been to Gwen's shop a few afternoons as well. That was a good thing. Maybe.

"Well?"

"None of your business."

She inhaled dramatically. "Nooooooo. Omigod. I don't even know what to say."

"Nothing. Say nothing."

"Okay, no need to panic. Really. Just don't panic."

"Not panicking," he said, as panic coursed through him. Dammit. His little sister was always complicating his life.

"Maybe they are really forgiving people. Aren't they churchy?"

He gripped the steering wheel, trying not to let his irritation show. "I'm not sure churchy is an actual thing."

She ignored him. "I'm curious to meet all these people. Are they all as nice as Gwen?"

"From what I can tell. They are kind of like the perfect family." He loved and hated that about them. It only added to his insecurity about his past and the secrets he was keeping.

"Great. That must make you feel better."

"Nothing wrong with our family," he said, turning onto the road that led to the Bailey's house.

"No, I know Mom was a total saint, I just mean the rest

of it. You know, the loser dad that walked out on us and left Mom broke with two small kids to raise?"

"Can't pick who our parents are, Haley. I'm not going to take on that burden and you shouldn't either." Hell, he had lots of things that were on him, a loser father wasn't one of them. But it still didn't help the situation because as an adult he'd made his own stupid mistakes.

"Doesn't it make you feel inferior though? Like when you're dating a woman who comes from a totally normal, wonderful family?"

"Uh, not till now. Thanks."

She laughed and patted his leg. "No, no, it's fine. Totally fine. The doctor thing helps you. People love doctors."

He inhaled slowly, wondering why he was engaging in conversation about his love life with his sister. They pulled into the driveway and Haley sighed.

"Even the prefect house," she whispered. "A Georgian in Montana," she said.

"Apparently, Gwen's mother lived in something like this when she was little and so Gwen's dad had it built for her."

"Wow."

"Yeah. So on the happy note of how inferior we are to the Baileys, would you like to go inside?"

She laughed and patted his shoulder. "It'll all be good. I'll keep referring to you as doctor tonight and I'll put in a plug or two about what a great big brother you are."

He tried to tune out Haley's jabbering because she only made him more nervous. He felt like a damn teenager. He couldn't remember the last time he'd met a woman's parents. Okay, so he'd technically already met them, but being invited to Sunday dinner was different. It was acknowledging that he was someone significant in their daughter's life. Hell. What the hell had he done?

Gwen opened the door, looking so beautiful, and so

genuinely happy to see him, that he resolved to make this right. He'd never been a guy who ran from the truth. In fact, he'd often been told he was too blunt, but what he'd let happen between him and Gwen was so uncharacteristic of him. She had lured him in and he'd fallen hard without even realizing it until he was in too deep.

"Hi, come on in," she said, tugging on his hand. "Haley, how are you?" she asked, taking his sister's jacket first.

"Great. Feeling so much more rested," his sister said. "My brother may be a total pain in the ass, but he's got a good heart. The best heart," she said, putting her arm around him in a totally uncharacteristic display of sibling loyalty.

"I know he does," Gwen said, laughing. She looked up at him, her eyes shining with everything she felt for him, and in that second, in that look in her brown eyes, he knew this couldn't go on. He would have to come clean today. After dinner he'd drop Haley off at his place and then go to Gwen's apartment.

Pretty soon the entire front entrance was filled with Gwen's family and introductions and small talk filled the elegant space.

"Let's all head to the dining room," Gwen's father said, extending his arm in the direction of the room on the left. "Cassie's been cooking up a storm all morning and Gwen has a dessert surprise that I'm not allowed to eat until we've had dinner, so hurry up, people."

They all laughed and made their way into the dining room. He wasn't hungry at all.

"I want to sit beside Luke," Maggie said, surprising him. He ignored the lump in his throat as he smiled down at the little girl.

"Well, honey, I'm sure he wants to sit beside Gwen and his sister," her father said.

"It's okay!" Haley said. "You sit beside him, sweetie. Tell

you the truth, I need a break from my big brother for a bit."

Maggie apparently thought this was hilarious. "Oh, I get you. I'm sure if I get a brother one day I'll need a break from him too."

They all laughed and he noticed the mischievous look between Chase and Julia. True enough, he sat down at the table, being treated like he was one of the family. Gwen was on his one side, her hand on his thigh, while Maggie was on his other side. "So, we have an announcement to make," Chase said, right before they were about to eat.

Gwen squeezed his hand and he heard a few gasps around the table from the women. Clearly they all had a handle on what was about to be announced, while the men all looked clueless.

"Ahem," Maggie said, clearing her throat theatrically for a few seconds.

"Right. Maggie has actually asked if she could make the announcement," Julia said, tugging on Chase's shirt and he sat down, smiling.

Maggie stood, looking very serious and pulled out a piece of paper from her Hello Kitty purse that was draped on the back of her chair. He made eye contact with his sister whom he could tell was getting a kick out of her like everyone else at the table. Maggie took a very long time unfolding the lined paper and then turned to slowly look at everyone in the room. "Maggs, hon, people want to eat their dinner," Chase said, clearly struggling to not laugh.

Maggie gave him a nod, cleared her throat, and then began reading. He could see from where he was sitting, she had taken a lot of effort and her printing was neat and in pencil. "I'm very happy today because I found out that my mom and dad— " She paused to point to Chase and Julia even though everyone knew who they were, but he suspected she did it for dramatic effect. She was impressive. "Are going to make me the proud owner of a little brother or sister."

Chase choked on his wine and the room erupted into shouts of laughter and cheers. Gwen had ditched him, alternating giving hugs to Chase and Julia and Maggie and then everyone else. He stood there, beside his sister, feeling their joy. He felt it seep inside him, mingling with his shame, his sorrow. These people had been through hell, and they were here, wholeheartedly embracing joy, embracing their future. Julia had lost her child, and now she'd had the courage to move forward and try again. It was something he couldn't understand.

"I'm so happy for them," Gwen said, coming back over to him as they all moved back to their seats. He awkwardly extended his congratulations as did his sister. He felt Haley's gaze, he felt what she wanted him to do. He couldn't do this tonight. He couldn't do it and ruin Chase and Julia's news. He couldn't do it with Maggie around.

Mrs. Bailey stood and everyone quieted. "Before we start eating, I want us to bow our heads. Lord, thank you for this food in front of us today, but thank you mostly for these new blessings you keep giving us. Thank you for these children that keep coming into our lives. Thank you for our new friends seated with us. Thank you for guiding us to the spring."

Jesus. Everyone started eating voraciously and he sat there, accepting platters and numbly passing them around. He had known they were a praying bunch, but this was too much. He'd caught the sniffles coming from his sister during the prayer and had avoided looking at her. Mrs. Bailey had given thanks for their new friends, him, and his sister. She had no idea that they would be her enemy.

Conversation flowed smoothly and lively but as the night went on he had an increasingly hard time participating or eating. His sister kept giving him the look and he could barely swallow the food.

"Are you okay?" Gwen asked quietly before the dessert course.

He turned to her, seeing the genuine concern in her brown eyes and then out at the people in the room, that sick feeling in his gut ready to consume him. He glanced over at his sister who was watching him. He knew what she was silently telling him to do. He'd wanted to do this in private, with Gwen first, but maybe this was the right way. They all needed to know. They were calling him a hero, they all thought he was some great guy.

"I was thinking maybe next weekend we could plan something special," Gwen said under her breath. The look in her eyes expressed everything that he'd been trying to avoid. They were getting too close. He couldn't sleep with her again, not without her knowing his real identity.

"Gwen," he said, finding it difficult to speak. "Can we talk?" he asked in a low voice.

Her eyes widened and he knew she was incorrectly assuming that he was dumping her. "Oh my god," she whispered.

"It's not what you think, but I need to talk to you. I haven't been completely honest with you."

It was at that moment that he noticed how eerily quiet the room had gotten. Heat climbed his neck as he saw the entire table staring at him.

"You can go ahead and say whatever it is you need to say now," Jack said, his voice holding an unmistakeable edge to it. Lily punched him.

"You can go into the kitchen and have privacy," her mother said, worry causing a frown between her brows. He glanced at his sister who was giving him the look.

He looked at Jack. He didn't want to do this in front of everyone. He wanted to speak to Gwen privately but he owed all of them the truth. "I'd rather speak to Gwen first."

Gwen took his hand and his gut churned at the sweetness of the gesture. She had no idea what he was going to say, but she was already taking his side.

"Jack, stop acting like a playground bully," she said, rolling her eyes at her brother. She turned to him. "There's no point in going into the kitchen, Luke, they're all just going to eavesdrop at the door."

He bit down hard on his teeth. This was torture. Her faith in him was torture. "I want to talk to you later. Tonight," he whispered.

Her smile faltered slightly.

"Out with it, because now you're making me think some bad thoughts about who you are or what you need to tell my sister," Jack said in a voice dripping with suspicion.

"He's not an escaped convict or ax-murderer," Haley hissed.

Ah, hell, now this was turning into a crap show. His sister was hotheaded. The entire situation was getting out of hand. He slowly pulled his hand from Gwen's and stood up. He was going to have to do this now.

"I haven't been honest with any of you about why I first came to Shadow Creek."

The once boisterous chatter now dimmed to nothing and everyone's eyes were on him and he could feel Gwen's gaze heating him. God, he was going to destroy her life. His biggest regret was getting involved with her.

"Didn't you come here to work at the hospital?" Edward Bailey asked, his eyes serious.

He nodded, meeting his gaze. "I came to Shadow Creek for another reason, but ended up working at the hospital when I found out about the doctor shortage out here."

"That's very commendable," Cassy said, giving him a nod and an encouraging smile. Her faith in him was humbling.

He cleared his throat and frantically thought of the speech

he'd prepared for years. He'd said it in front of the mirror, on the drive to work, when going to bed at night. And yet now he struggled with the words he knew by heart. "About five years ago, I had accepted a job at the hospital outside of Shadow Creek. I had pulled a double shift at the hospital and was exhausted. I shouldn't have been driving that night, but I needed to get back to check in on my mother who was very sick at the time. My wife who…" He paused again, looked down. Shame and regret poured through him, unrelenting. His knuckles turned white as he clutched the chair. "She was six months pregnant was beside me in the car. We were arguing. The roads were slick and visibility was next to nothing with the fog and freezing rain."

"Omigod," Julia whispered holding her head in her hands.

He refused to picture it, the image that was burned in his memory, of the wreckage.

"When was this?" Julia whispered.

He stared across the table at the woman that he'd perhaps taken the most from and told her the exact date, cringing at the gasps around the table, at the tears that immediately filled her eyes. "The reason I came to Shadow Creek was to meet all of you and to apologize for taking two important people from your lives." There, he said it, but relief didn't come.

Self-loathing sliced through him as they stared at him, as the reality of what he signified in their lives sank in. There had been so many days he'd forced himself to crawl out of bed, to try and bury his shame and continue living. But there had been so many more days where he'd allowed the self-hatred to rip a hole inside him. None of it had adequately prepared him for facing these people.

Jack stood abruptly, but Lily grabbed hold of him, urging him to sit down.

"What do you mean, Luke? There were no charges laid that night." Chase said.

"I know. I wasn't charged with anything because technically it was just poor road conditions. But I know it was my fault. I was tired. I was distracted. We were arguing. I should have been driving slower. My car spun off the road and down the cliff. I thought that was it. As we went over, I knew there was no way any of us should survive that fall. But I did." He still didn't know why. He didn't understand how he had walked away without a scratch. He hated that he had. There had been so many days where he'd wished he hadn't survived. He hadn't deserved to survive over everyone who'd died. The Bailey's son, their grandson. His wife. Their baby. Sometimes he'd wondered if that was his destiny and he would just have to live out the rest of his life as the man who'd killed so many beloved people. But then he'd met Gwen and he'd allowed himself to stupidly, pathetically, think that maybe he deserved more.

"Finish your story," Jack said. The tension in his face was obvious, his voice laced with accusation.

Luke ran his hand over his jaw, relief and shame pouring into him at the same time "My car spun off the road and down the cliff."

"How the hell did you survive that?"

Luke shrugged. "I don't know. I'm sorry. I just know that I have wished every single day that it had been me. I know how important that little boy…" When his voice broke and his eyes filled with tears he paused. "I know that little boy and his father meant the world to all of you. I'm sorry. That's all I have to offer, but know that I regret every day what happened that night."

"You should have told us right away who you were," Jack said.

He nodded, turning to Jack. "I know. I was working my way up to telling you. I hadn't planned on getting involved with Gwen. I tried to fight my feelings and just remain indifferent. But I fell in love with her. I should have come clean, but by that point I couldn't lose her either."

"Let's be clear, man, you didn't cause that accident," Chase said.

"I know." He knew that. Technically. But he blamed himself.

In his last days with his mother, when the bad just kept getting worse, he'd brought her home to his house. He and Haley had spent every moment with her, cherishing her, and telling her what a wonderful mother she'd been to them. On that last night, he'd lain beside her in bed, the faint glow from the television and the news on low, keeping him company while his mother slept, her breath low, very shallow. At some point during the night, he'd drifted into a light sleep, but she woke him with a featherlight touch. "Don't ever doubt why you're still here, Luke."

Her eyes had been clear, she was completely lucid despite the pain meds.

He had shaken his head, disagreeing.

"No. You must find a way to forgive yourself. You must find a way to trust that there are other plans being made for your life, Luke. But you are meant to be here. Don't waste it," she'd whispered, reaching out for him. He'd grasped her thin hand and wept, holding on to her, on to her words, on to their last moments together.

Luke blinked, aware that he must have paused, the memory of that night resurfacing unexpectedly. He stared at all of them, hating that his mother had been wrong. Luke ran his hand over his jaw, relief and shame pouring into him at the same time "I'm sorry."

He stood there, motionless, until Maggie stood up. His heart slammed against his chest as she wrapped her arms around his waist. "It's okay, you didn't mean to."

"Maggie," Chase said harshly, his face white.

Gwen was holding her head in her hands, refusing to look at him. The room was engulfed in silence again. The scrape of a chair, then Gwen's mother standing. His heart started beating furiously as she crossed the room. He didn't know what she was going to do, and he could tell no one else did either.

His composure threatened to crumble when she took her hand in his for a moment, her eyes filled with tears... and forgiveness and something he just didn't get. "You've suffered, Luke. It was not your fault. You have suffered that burden long enough."

He squeezed his eyes shut and hugged the woman whose life he'd destroyed. He hugged her, trying to accept the gift she was giving him, even though he knew he didn't deserve it. It wasn't what he was expecting. The grace she was showing humbled him and as she clung to him, he let her warmth comfort him, reminding him of his own mother.

Julia stood next and walked over to him.

"I'm so sorry, Julia," he said in a voice so raw that it hurt to speak.

"I know," she whispered, crying. "I know." Then she wrapped her arms around him. Nothing in his life had been more overwhelming than this, standing in front of these people, having them forgive him. But Gwen and Jack didn't stand up.

Her father stood and walked over to him, placing his hand on his shoulder and gripping hard. "You've got to let it go, son. It wasn't your fault."

• • •

Gwen looked over at Jack. He was watching her. Neither of them stood. She couldn't quite catch her breath, the deep burn of betrayal making it impossible.

She felt deceived.

She felt Luke's pain, his guilt, and on a level she couldn't quite reach. Instead, she started thinking about how they first met, all the times he'd helped her…it had been out of guilt. She thought he'd walked into her shop and it was destiny… but it wasn't. It had all been planned by him.

Was the reason he'd taken time off work to help her through the flu all because he felt he owed her family? He'd never told her that. Those five years of his life had been missing. He'd kept a major part of himself from her. She thought he'd been so amazing when he'd helped her with the flu, but it had been guilt. The night of the singles dating…again it had been pity. How could she have been so incredibly stupid? None of this had been about her or them; it had all been about his guilt. It all made sense why he never told her—it was because it would reveal his true motive.

She could tell he was trying to keep it together. Maybe this all meant she was a horrible person. Everyone in the room had forgiven him, but she sat here incapable of finding forgiveness. It was the utter humiliation of being used. The pain of knowing it was all for nothing.

She felt his sister's gaze and Gwen refused to look at her. She knew Haley was expecting her to get up and forgive him, but she couldn't.

"I need to speak to you privately," Gwen finally managed to say, not quite looking into Luke's eyes. The room went silent and Luke gave her a nod. She stiffened when she felt the light touch of his hand at the small of her back. Just a mere hour ago that touch would have been welcome, it would have sent shivers of delight through her body. Now it was just a reminder of what an idiot she'd been.

She walked out of the dining room, aware of the silence amongst a group of people who were never silent, and through the kitchen out onto the back deck. The cold air was a welcome balm on her overheated face. She looked up at Luke as he stood there, his hands in his pockets, the lines around his mouth in a deep frown.

"Why would you do this?" she asked, feeling numb.

He gave a rough sigh. "I never meant to hurt you. I never meant to fall in love with you," he said, wincing. Love. He loved her.

She groaned and covered her face for a moment. "Stop lying to me."

He took a step closer. "I'm not lying."

"Like you haven't been lying to me this past month, right?"

She turned from the grief in his eyes.

"I didn't. It just happened. Think back to the beginning. I went out of my way to make sure we wouldn't get involved."

"You walked into my shop. You sat at a table there for over two months."

"I didn't know who you were at first. By the time I found out, I was hooked on you. There was something about you, your smile, your laugh. I needed it so badly. I swore to myself it would be hands off, but the night of the storm, when you were crying, that was it. I kept wanting to tell you."

It was absurd. "All those nice things you did for me, was it just pity?"

"I couldn't pity you. You're the most amazing, together, woman I know."

Clearly, he needed to get out more. She turned from the heartbreaking picture he made. "What happened the night of the accident?"

"I've already told you."

She shut her eyes and remembered what he'd said about the accident, clinging to the possibility that maybe it wasn't as bad as she thought. "What I don't get is why you blamed yourself. You weren't drinking, you weren't texting, what made you take on the blame?"

He rubbed a hand over his jaw. "I shouldn't have gotten behind the wheel. I was dead tired, and I was distracted. I'd pulled a double shift. Lisa and I didn't have a great relationship. We didn't want kids. Her getting pregnant was an accident. We were so self-absorbed that we didn't appreciate what we'd been given. We were arguing about who was going to have to adjust their work schedule to accommodate the baby, whether or not we were going to have to get a live-in nanny. So that's the rest of it. I blame myself for not loving that baby, for that baby dying without ever thinking her parents loved her. I blamed myself for surviving while a dad and kid died. I hated myself."

She cried as the pain and shame in his voice reverberated through her. The ultrasound picture she'd found in his wallet. Oh God, it was too much. If this had happened any other way, she'd be offering him compassion. She wanted to reach out and comfort him, to tell him none of it was his fault, but what good would that do? The air between them was so thick, so heavy, she could barely breathe. She couldn't process what was happening. It was as though he was a different man than the one she'd come to know this last month.

Gwen leaned her head against the wall, wishing there was a way out of this. But how would she ever look at him the same? And how could she trust him again? How did she even trust his feelings for her? What if he'd just felt sorry for her this entire time? She was the girl who'd never gotten her life back together after her brother and nephew died. She had gone and fallen in love with someone who had lied to her.

"Gwen," he said in that deep voice that seemed to fill all her dreams every night.

"Please go," she whispered, struggling not to break down. "Please go and live your life away from me. I can't ever look at you the same way. I can't trust you. You made me the family idiot. Gwen finally finds a guy and he turns out to be the one who caused the car accident that killed…omigod," she said, starting to sob into her hands. "It's all so messed up. Just leave me alone."

Pain slashed across his handsome features, his jaw tight, his eyes so wounded she had to turn away. She hated herself right now, she hated that she used that against him, but her pride kept her from breaking down in front of him.

"You're right."

She snapped her head up and looked at him. She hadn't expected that.

"I screwed this up. This is why I never wanted to get involved with you or anyone else. I'm not the guy to bet on. I'm not the guy you need. Nothing I felt for you was fake, all of it was so damn real and that's what makes this so hard. I spent the last five years hating myself. I wished I'd been the one who died. I would have traded places in a second to give you all back the people you lost. But I can't. It's taken me five years to be able to stand here today and confess this, to say how sorry I am. I will never be able to give you your brother or nephew back. I will never get my wife or baby back. All I know is that for some reason I walked into your shop that first day. Your smile was the first thing in five years that made me thankful for being alive. I fell in love with you against my better judgment. Loving you was so damn good that I hid my identity because I would rather have whatever you were willing to give me, for however long, than not have you at all. All of it was real. Every word I said to you, everything that happened our night together was real."

Gwen kept wiping the tears that were falling down her face. She ached for him. She ached for the man that felt such guilt for being alive, for the burden he'd had on his shoulders. She hated that he thought his life was less valuable then everyone else's. But what she hated most of all was the fact that she couldn't reach out and hug him and offer him forgiveness. She hated that she was going to let him walk away.

. . .

Gwen didn't want to go back inside and face everyone. She wished she could just escape out the back door, go back to her place and hide. She could just imagine the looks of pity from Julia and Lily. She wrapped her hands around the deck railing and took a deep breath, trying to compose herself before she went back inside.

She dug her palms into her eyes and balled all over again. How cruel could life be? As if the last five years hadn't been hard enough. Now the one guy she actually… loved had been the driver of the car that had killed Michael and Matthew. And not just that—let her fall in love with him without ever revealing his identity?

She stiffened when she heard the patio door open. She didn't know which of her family members to expect. She looked over to see her mother sitting down beside her; she was wrapped up in her winter coat, hat, and gloves. "I don't understand why my children insist on sitting on this back porch in the winter."

Gwen tried to smile, to make some vain attempt at looking like she wasn't falling apart.

"So, Luke and his sister left."

Gwen shrugged.

"Gwen, he's in pain. He has suffered. He lost everything—his wife, his job, his entire life. He has paid the ultimate price and he still hasn't forgiven himself."

The image of him standing in front of her family, telling them what had happened made her ache. "I know. I just. I can't look at him. I'll never be able to look at him and forget. He's the reason Michael and Matthew are gone. How will I ever be able to live with that?"

Her mother took her hand. "He's not the reason. He was the other driver. He was not the reason they died. We will never know why the Lord called them home."

She turned from her mother. She couldn't get into this religious stuff now. There was faith and then there was... just deferring everything to God when they didn't have the answers. "So, what, if someone gets murdered, that person isn't accountable and it was God calling them home?"

Her mother sighed. "I don't have all the answers, but don't you dare try and insinuate that Matthew and Michael were murdered that night. We are hearing from a man who has blamed himself for too long. Gwen, he stopped living."

"He admitted he was responsible."

"And then he pulled me out of deep waters," her mother said.

Gwen threw up her hands. "I don't want to hear it!" She covered her ears for a moment. "How can you stand there and quote the bible to me? It was that man who ran into their car. There was no water, no one pulled anyone out. They all died."

"I don't think that's what you mean to say. I don't think you blame him for that accident at all."

"I don't know what I think."

"What I think, Gwen, is that you feel very deeply for Luke. I know the deep compassion you have for people—it is one of your most admirable traits. You feel. You want to help people in need, you always have. I think you are aching for the pain that man is dealing with day in and day out. But I think the issue here is that you're upset because he didn't tell you the truth. Or are you upset because you doubt if he really had feelings for you and you're now thinking back to everything he's done and that it was all motivated by guilt and pity?"

How her mother knew this stuff was beyond her. Yes, to all of the above. She didn't say anything for a long while, just stood there with her arms crossed, staring at her mother beside her. How many times during her childhood had her mother been right about things? How many times had she guided her and her brothers to a peaceful resolution of arguments? Heck, she'd even guided Jack into finally reconciling what had happened.

"Well, how would you feel about Luke? About welcoming him into this family?"

"He's a good man. I know he's a good man. If he wasn't, he wouldn't have been in Shadow Creek for half a year worrying about us, talking to us. He wouldn't have left his home in order to ask our forgiveness. If he wasn't a good man, he wouldn't have lost everything. If he wasn't a good man, he would have walked away from that accident without thinking twice about any of us. He wasn't charged, Gwen. He didn't do anything wrong. He's a man who's taken on this burden. Day in and day out that man has to live with the fact that his wife and unborn baby died, another man and child died. How does he live with that kind of guilt?"

She swiped the tears rolling down her face, knowing her mother was right. He had suffered so much.

"He told me he didn't know how he walked out of his car that night. He had no idea how he survived his car going over that ridge. The impact of the fall should have killed him instantly."

It was awful to think about on so many levels, but especially on the one that she loved him. "What do I do?" she asked.

"Forgive him. First in your heart, forgive him. Then go to him and tell him you forgive him as many times as it takes until he believes you, and until you're sure he forgives himself. You'll never have a future with him if he doesn't believe you or if he still hasn't forgiven himself."

"And you would be okay with this? You'd be okay seeing him every day? What about Jack? What about Julia? How would they feel?"

"Gwen, Julia went up to him and hugged him."

"Jack didn't," she said, remembering the look on her brother's face.

"It takes him longer to process. He'll come around, I know he will."

She ran her hands through her hair. "I can't be you, Mom. I can't do what you do." She shut her eyes as she remembered the night they'd slept together. He'd kept so much from her and she'd given him all of her, her body, her heart, her soul. "I can't be with a man who would lie to me like that, no matter what the reasons are. He even told me he wasn't the right man for me. He walked away."

"You're not being fair. Of course he doesn't think he's right for you—he doesn't think he deserves you. He walked away because you turned him away and he doesn't blame you for it."

"Well, whatever his reasons were, I don't think I can get past this," she whispered. She covered her face and felt her mother's arms come around her. For the first time in a very long time she let herself be the one who was comforted.

Chapter Eleven

Luke paused as he crossed the hospital parking lot on his way to his car. The figure standing in front of it was familiar, but not the one he was hoping to see, especially after the double shift he'd just pulled. He'd been working a lot of extra hours to not think about Gwen.

He resumed walking and waved to Jack Bailey.

"Hi," Jack said. He didn't know Gwen's brother well. He did have deep respect and admiration for the man who'd risked his life to save Lily and their unborn babies. He'd first met Jack the night of the snowstorm when Jack had walked miles to get Lily to a hospital.

Jack was the only other person besides Gwen the night of his confession to not offer any forgiveness. He didn't blame him.

Luke tossed his bag into the trunk, not saying anything, not knowing what this was about.

"You have a couple minutes?" Jack asked. His hands were in the front pockets of his jeans, his eyes, so like Gwen's, serious.

Luke gave him a nod, bracing himself.

"I spent the last five years angry and living in my own self-imposed hell. I walked away from everyone I loved. I almost lost all of them. I blamed myself for my brother and nephew's deaths, too."

Luke looked down at the ground, not knowing what to say.

"I realized, way too late, that it wasn't my fault. It was just one of those things that happens. But I was angry for a long time and I left my family. I have them all back now. I'm about to be a father. I'm not going to welcome my kids into the world holding on to anger."

Luke looked up at him, meeting his serious gaze.

Jack gave him a nod. "Yeah. I can't say I came to this decision quickly or on my own," he said, the corner of his mouth turning up slightly.

Luke rubbed his hands over his jaw. "Thank you. I, uh, didn't expect that."

Jack shrugged. "I think you've blamed yourself enough, man. You're welcome here. No one blames you. Not even me. So, if you want to date my sister…or whatever…you have my blessing."

Luke looked down, clearing his throat. The weight he'd been carrying for so long, slowly lifting, slowly clearing. "Thank you. I don't actually think Gwen is speaking to me right now."

Jack cracked a smile. "Yeah, she's pretty stubborn. She's a softie though. She'll come around I'm sure."

He didn't think so.

"Give her some time. I'm sure Lily, Julia, and my mother will work on her. I will say this, if you hurt her, you'll have me to answer to. But, even scarier than me, you'll have her to answer to. She can fight. She holds a grudge. You will regret ever letting her down, because even worse than her best punch, is the look of disappointment in her eyes."

His gut churned because he'd seen that look, and it had hurt.

• • •

One week later, Gwen was busy wallowing in self-pity when a knock at the door interrupted her miserable thoughts. She quickly pulled the two large casserole dishes from the oven and set them on the counter before answering the door.

At first her heart skipped a few beats thinking it might be Luke, but then that would just complicate things. She knew in her heart that she was going to have to go to him, but she was stalling. Did she blame him for the car accident? No. Not at all. She felt sorry for him, that he'd blamed himself all these years, that he'd tortured himself for something that was truly an accident.

So the only reason she hadn't gone to him was the niggling self-doubt about their relationship. It bothered her that he'd kept it from her. It bothered her that it made her doubt the sincerity of his feelings toward her. She needed to make her move though. Maybe she was waiting for a sign, a final thing that would push her into action.

She hadn't heard from him since he'd walked out of her parents' house. She had taken all the shifts at the Chocolaterie, trying to get her mind off him but it hadn't worked. He, obviously hadn't been by either. In her free time she was cooking up a storm. Apparently Bri said her kids loved all her cooking, so she'd volunteered to bring over some extra freezer meals today.

She took a deep breath and opened the door. It was Haley.

"Hi, I'm so sorry for just dropping by. Can I come in?"

She held the door open for Haley and let her in. She smiled at her. "No problem. Come on in. Can I get you anything?"

Haley took off her coat and sat on the barstool at the kitchen island. "What smells so good?"

Gwen smiled at her, noticing again how similar she and Luke looked. "Oh, I'm just making some food for a friend. Do you like homemade mac 'n' cheese?"

Her pretty face lit up. Gwen scooped a generous serving into a bowl. Haley began inhaling it. Her heart squeezed when she remembered Luke doing the same thing a couple weeks ago. He *had* tried to avoid a relationship. Now all of his weird standoffish behavior made sense. "How are you doing?"

Haley smiled and wiped her mouth. "I'm okay, except my brother is driving me insane."

Her stomach toppled around. "Oh, really?"

Haley nodded. "He's moping. Then he's working. Then he comes home and mopes some more. He hasn't even wanted to eat pizza. I actually think I'm going to leave for a few days. Maybe visit friends and give him some space."

Gwen crossed her arms. "I…uh, have been meaning to go see him."

Haley let out a dramatic gust of air and dragged her fork around the bowl, trying to snag some cheese remnants. "Oh thank God. Seriously, he's a disaster without you."

She really shouldn't feel happiness. "Really?"

Haley leaned forward, nodding repeatedly. "He loves you so much."

Tears stung her eyes. "I don't know why it took me so long to see him. I don't blame him for the accident, Haley. I hate thinking that he believes that."

"Because you're worried he pitied you. I get that. Totally. I even tried explaining it to him, but he didn't get it. He's…I totally get why you're mad at him. But, Gwen…" Her voice trailed and her eyes filled with tears. "You don't know. You don't know what he's been through, how he's tortured himself. I didn't think I'd ever get my brother back, but seeing him with you, you brought him back. You made him think he deserved another chance. Now…I know he wants to leave Shadow Creek for good. He looks like he used to before he met you and it's killing me to see him like this."

Gwen handed her a tissue and grabbed one for herself. She didn't know what to say to Haley, but she knew she needed to get to him. She had stayed silent long enough. She knew in her heart that Luke was a good man. Maybe she'd known all along…from her first encounter with her Muffin Man, she'd known he was special. He didn't deserve to feel any more pain. He needed to know she didn't blame him. "Okay…I'm going to shower and then go see him."

"Perfect!" Haley said, bouncing off the chair and standing. "I'm going to visit a friend for the weekend and I'll get out of your hair."

She shook her head. "Oh, don't feel like you need to leave on my account."

Haley waved a hand. "No, seriously, I'm leaving because he needs a break from me…or I need a break from him," she said with a laugh. She leaned forward and gave her a quick hug. "Good luck!"

· · ·

Luke opened the door, ready to chastise his sister for forgetting her keys again, but blinked as he saw Gwen standing there.

A little piece of heaven on his doorstep.

He wasn't so naïve to believe that she was there to forgive him, so he didn't think about that. Instead he just looked at her. She was more beautiful than he remembered. Staying away from her this week had been a new kind of hell for him; thinking about her hating him had almost been too much to handle. But she was there now, her shiny hair blowing around her with the wind. Her dark eyes were filled with secrets, but no blame, no hatred for him.

"Hi," she finally said. "I brought you a giant dish of mac 'n' cheese as a peace offering."

He swallowed hard past the lump in his throat and stepped into her, the casserole dish between them. Her head tilted back and her eyes were shiny, and he spoke the only words that he could muster up. "God, baby, I don't need a peace offering, I don't need a damn thing in this world except you." He leaned down and kissed her, capturing her sigh, her essence. He kissed her with all his regrets, his love, and his gratitude. He kissed her, knowing he was never going to lose her again.

When the stupid casserole dish almost fell because she raised her hands to clutch his shoulders, he broke the kiss. She came inside and he placed the dish on the hall table.

"I was coming here to tell you that I love you and I don't blame you. I know it was an accident. You have to forgive yourself, Luke."

He shut his eyes and finally allowed forgiveness to come to him. It had been a long time. But the woman wrapped up in his arms, the woman he'd almost lost, was offering him her heart and he knew to make it okay he was going to have to forgive himself. "Thank you," he whispered, leaning forward to kiss her again. He unbuttoned her coat while he kissed her and what started as a slow and poignant kiss became frantic. They began a mad dash for clothes removal in between kisses.

"Your sister isn't coming back for a while," she said as he backed her up against the door and locked it.

He kissed the soft spot just below her ear, smiling as she shivered. "Oh, that's good. I was planning on locking her out since she always forgets her keys."

Gwen laughed against his mouth. "That's awful."

"I know. Now I won't have to feel awful and great at the same time." He had her clothes off in record time and she managed the same with him.

"Wait," she whispered before he kissed her again.

He stopped, looking down at her.

"This time," she said, raising her hands to frame his face. "This time we do this, I want you to know how much I love you, Luke. All of you. Your past, your present. The man you are today. I love you."

He squeezed his eyes shut as gratitude shook him. Gwen was life's biggest gift to him. She'd dragged him out of the hell he'd been living in and given him a new life. He leaned down and kissed her, vowing to show her, with his lips, his body, his hands, just how much he adored her.

• • •

Gwen woke up sometime during the night very aware that she was somewhere warm and safe. Sure enough, she opened her eyes and Luke was under her. He smiled at her. She realized she'd never get tired of looking at him. Her Muffin Man was even more gorgeous than she thought that first day she'd met him. Now, knowing who he really was, knowing what he'd been through, made him so much more beautiful to her.

"Have you been awake this whole time?"

He shrugged as a smile tugged at the corner of his gorgeous mouth. "It's a bit difficult to sleep with you lying on top of me."

"Oh," she whispered, her eyes going to his mouth. "You're very toasty."

He choked out a laugh. "So are you."

"So what happens now, Luke?"

He grinned, a slow, sexy grin. "What do you want to happen now?"

She laughed. "I mean, what do we do about all our problems? You're leaving."

"Haley said she'll stay in Shadow Creek if I will."

"Wow." She didn't want to ask what that meant.

"I want to stay, Gwen. I want to stay with you," he said, his hands coming up to frame her face. "Wherever you are, I am. If you're sure that's what you want. If you're sure that you can look at me and not see me as the reason for your brother and nephew's death."

The question coupled with the vulnerability in such a strong, masculine face, made her chest ache. She felt so badly for making him think that she blamed him. Her eyes filled with tears. "You weren't responsible. You weren't. I don't blame you. No one blames you. You are a good man. Your wife, your baby…I know you," she whispered. In that sweet way of hers, she looked at him, placing her hand on his heart. "I know the real you. You have a good heart."

He squeezed his eyes shut as she pressed her lips to his chest, his heart beating painfully. He was ready to accept her faith in him, in their future, in the person she believed him to be.

He kissed her, welcoming the place she was taking him to, welcoming his redemption.

Epilogue

"Thank you, everyone, for coming tonight and helping us celebrate our wedding day. I want to thank all of you who are here, and those who are watching us from above."

Luke swallowed past the lump of emotion in his throat as he took his bride's hand and paused. Gwen was smiling at him, joy palpating from her body as she stood beside him at the podium. They were standing in his in-law's garden, in a gazebo that had been erected for their wedding day. Tents had been set up and twinkling lights lit them and the summer sky. Massive bouquets of roses and hydrangeas were in the center of the round tables.

His gaze went from Gwen's beautiful face to the crowd again, landing on that table in the front that was filled with people he was grateful and proud and humbled to call family. The Baileys all sat there, some of them laughing, some crying, and some drinking. But all of them, had his back. He winked at his sister who sat amongst them all, as though she'd known them a lifetime, as though she was family. Maybe that was what was so amazing about them, they had given him and his sister family, when they were both adults, when they thought they were past the age of needing family.

They accepted him, they forgave him, and they freed him.

But it was the woman holding his hand who had given him back his faith.

He looked back down at her, knowing none of this was an accident. He knew he was meant to love Gwen. Her brown eyes sparkled and she nudged her chin in the direction of his speech, a subtle reminder that he hadn't finished. But he wasn't feeling hurried tonight, so he leaned down and gave her a long kiss, smiling against her mouth as the crowd cheered. When he finally pulled his mouth from hers, he kissed her on the forehead and looked back out at the people who filled the tent, not needing to look at the words, already knowing them.

"I want to thank my sister, Hayley, for being the best little sister a guy could ever ask for. You never lost your faith in me, and I owe you one," he said, giving her a wink and raising his glass. "I've got your back, forever." His sister ruined the moment by blowing her nose loudly as Maggie patted her back.

"To my new in-laws, and family. Thank you for taking me in, for making me one of your own. But most of all, thank you for giving me this incredible woman. I will spend the rest of my life loving her and honoring her."

With the cheers and all the glasses of champagne raised, Gwen grabbed his hand and they flew onto the dance floor. He hated dancing. He always had. But tonight wasn't about any of that. It was about Gwen. He drew her into his arms, feeling the weight that had been crushing him for almost six years, completely lifted.

"Wait till you see the cake," she whispered, a mischievous glint in her eyes as she stared up at him.

He smiled, having learned not to underestimate her. "I'm not really caring about the cake. Right now, I'm kind of wondering when we get to leave."

"Oh, trust me, you'll want the cake," she said.

His fingers grazed the fabric-covered buttons on the back of her silk gown, and he tried not to get carried away imagining what it was going to be like later, plucking them open one by one. Gwen was so beautiful tonight. She'd wanted the traditional wedding and he wasn't going to ruin her dream. It suited her perfectly. As the song ended, the Baileys crashed the dance floor and surrounded them.

Maggie barrelled into them and he picked her up, his bond with the little girl always surprising him. "The cake is coming," she whispered loudly.

He turned and he spotted two servers wheeling something out. Gasps and whispers from the guests made him curious now. He started laughing as he spotted the giant cake in the shape of a muffin. It was decorated with flowers and scrolly things and looked elegant, but it had the unmistakable likeness of a muffin.

"So Gwen finally married her Muffin Man," Jack said, slapping him on the shoulder.

He laughed at his brother-in-law. Chase came to stand on the other side of him. He felt completely at ease with both, often joining them when they met at The Roadhouse. The only person missing from this crowd was Hayley. He frowned, as he noticed she was standing next to a large, tough-looking guy at the bar.

"Who's that?" he asked aloud.

Jack glanced in the direction he pointed. "Oh, that's, uh, a good friend of mine from my oil-rigging days."

He stifled his hesitation. Last thing his sister needed was some other thug in her life. Before he could dwell on that, Gwen's parents came up to him and embraced him. He hugged them back, that feeling of peace coursing through him.

"Okay, so me and TMM need to go cut the cake," Gwen

said, barrelling through the circle. "And I think poor Lily deserves the first piece," she said.

They all turned to Lily who kinda looked like she was ready to explode with those twins. "I'm fine, I'm fine, but I totally appreciate the sentiment," she said with a laugh.

As they all walked toward the cake, he pulled Gwen toward the gazebo. He held her hand as she lifted one part of her dress off the grass. "I wanted to tell you one more thing," he said, pulling her close.

She shook her head, looking up at him with an adoration that was mutual. "You've said more and given me more than I ever dreamed," she whispered.

He cleared his throat and looked down at her. "I forgot to tell you about something else you were right about. Love at first sight. What I felt for you was love at first sight."

She inhaled sharply and clutched the front of his jacket. "Don't lie."

He grinned. "No lie. It just took me a while to figure it out."

She leaned into him and he kissed her for what had to be the twentieth time that day, but he never grew tired of it, of her. He could never get enough of Gwen. She was the woman he was meant to start over with, to live the life he wanted with. Gwen made him into the man he was supposed to be. The one his mother knew existed all those years ago.

He wrapped his arms around her, holding on tight, to life, to her love.

About the Author

Victoria James is a romance writer living near Toronto. She is a mother to two young children, one very disorderly feline, and wife to her very own hero.

Victoria attended Queen's University and graduated with a degree in English Literature. She then earned a degree in Interior Design. After the birth of her first child she began pursuing her life-long passion of writing.

Her dream of being a published romance author was realized by Entangled in 2012. Victoria is living her dream—staying home with her children and conjuring up happy endings for her characters.

Victoria would love to hear from her readers! You can visit her at www.victoriajames.ca or Twitter @vicjames101 or send her an email at Victoria@victoriajames.ca.

Discover the **Shadow Creek, Montana** *series…*

CHRISTMAS WITH THE SHERIFF

THE BABY BOMBSHELL

Also by Victoria James

THE RANCHER'S SECOND CHANCE

THE BEST MAN'S BABY

A RISK WORTH TAKING

THE DOCTOR'S FAKE FIANCÉE

RESCUED BY THE RNCHER

FALLING FOR THE P.I.

FALLING FOR HER ENEMY

THE REBEL'S RETURN

THE BILLIONAIRE'S CHRISTMAS BABY

THE BILLIONAIRE'S CHRISTMAS PROPOSAL

Find your Bliss with these great releases...

THE NANNY ARRANGEMENT
a *Country Blues* novel by Rachel Harris

Hannah is determined to make the man she's loved her entire life finally see her as a woman, with the help of a makeover and the convenient forced proximity of a tour bus. Deacon loves having his best friend on tour with him as his son's nanny, but he's afraid to rock the boat and lose the person most important in his life. One thing's for certain—their story would make one heck of a country song.

FROM FAKE TO FOREVER
a novel by Jennifer Shirk

Sandra Moyer's preschool is struggling, so she reluctantly agrees to let super-famous actor Ben Capshaw research a role there. Ben's always joking around, never serious, but there's something about the buttoned-up, beautiful Sandra and her young daughter that makes him want to take life more seriously. But Sandra won't trust him—what if it's all an act, research for the role? As the lines between make-believe and reality blur, Ben will have to decide if love is worth casting aside the role of his life for a new role...that could last a lifetime.

Falling for the Best Man
a *Sisters of Wishing Bridge* novel by Amanda Ashby

All Christopher Henderson wants is to find a fake girlfriend so his bosses think the bad boy has settled down and he can get his dream job. And what better place to find said companion, than at a wholesome vintage wedding. But he didn't count on seeing wedding planner Emmy Watson, the woman who dumped him. The one he hasn't been able to get off his mind. There's no denying the spark between them, but he's a globetrotter, and she's a homebody, and falling in love is something neither of them ever wants to do.

The Playboy's Proposal
a *Sorensen* novel by Ashlee Mallory

Doctor Benny Sorensen has had it up to here with her party-throwing playboy neighbor. She's declaring war. Wealthy ad man Henry Ellison lives an uncomplicated life that revolves around work, women, and partying. In that order. But when his attractive but hotheaded neighbor creates trouble for him, Henry offers to help her land a date with the man of her dreams. Only as Henry makes her over and coaches her on the fine art of flirting, he realizes that the idea of this woman in any other man's arms but his own is unacceptable.

Made in the USA
Monee, IL
16 May 2020